"The brake," Amy whispered, suddenly realizing why their team of horses had not bolted in fear.

She jumped out of the coach and threw herself up toward the driver's seat and loosened the brake.

If the road ran for a mile or two without a sharp turn, then she just might survive. But if not . . .

Just up ahead, she saw the road curve around the side of a mountain. One of the horses tried to squat down on his haunches and arrest the momentum of the coach, but he lost his footing and was dragged down.

"No!" Amy cried in horror as the coach ran over the falling horse and went airborne . . .

DON'T MISS THESE
ALL-ACTION WESTERN SERIES
FROM THE BERKLEY PUBLISHING GROUP

THE GUNSMITH by J. R. Roberts
>Clint Adams was a legend among lawmen, outlaws, and ladies. They called him . . . the Gunsmith.

LONGARM by Tabor Evans
>The popular long-running series about U.S. Deputy Marshal Long—his life, his loves, his fight for justice.

LONE STAR by Wesley Ellis
>The blazing adventures of Jessica Starbuck and the martial arts master Ki. Over eight million copies in print.

SLOCUM by Jake Logan
>Today's longest-running action Western. John Slocum rides a deadly trail of hot blood and cold steel.

WESLEY ELLIS

LONE STAR

AND THE NEVADA GOLD

JOVE BOOKS, NEW YORK

LONE STAR AND THE NEVADA GOLD

A Jove Book / published by arrangement with
the author

PRINTING HISTORY
Jove edition / November 1994

ISBN: 0-515-11494-4

A JOVE BOOK®
Jove Books are published by The Berkley Publishing Group,
200 Madison Avenue, New York, New York 10016.
JOVE and the "J" design are trademarks
belonging to Jove Publications, Inc.

PRINTED IN THE UNITED STATES OF AMERICA

10 9 8 7 6 5 4 3 2 1

Chapter 1

Jessica Starbuck gazed out the window of a first-class traveling compartment on the Union Pacific Railroad, her green eyes studying the vast reaches of the Nevada desert. Somewhere out here, she thought, was the answer to the mystery that had brought her rushing all the way from Texas and now she must unlock that mystery and help her dear friend, Amy Ross.

It had been almost two weeks since Jessica had received an urgent-sounding letter from Amy begging for assistance. The letter had been short and had posed far more questions than it had answered, but Jessica could not have failed to miss the desperation in Amy's last few lines, which read:

> *My father and my brother have both*
> *vanished as if from the face of the earth.*
> *Only last month, I heard that they were rich*
> *men with a tremendous new gold strike*
> *somewhere in the heart of the Nevada desert.*

*But now, everyone says that they must be dead
and that their gold mine never existed. I
don't care about the mine but my father and
brother mean everything to me. Please, help!*

Jessica had called in her faithful samurai friend, Ki,
and had shown him Amy's letter. She had asked one
question of the samurai: "Can we leave for Nevada
tomorrow?"

To which Ki had replied, "We can leave within the
hour, if your affairs are in order."

Jessica's affairs had been in order because she
was careful to keep them that way. Her late father,
Alex Starbuck, had left her heiress to the immense
Starbuck empire, which included mines, plantations, and
manufacturing enterprises around the world. But Jessie's
real love was her huge Texas ranch where she preferred to
spend most of her time, when not being forced to travel
because of business or grave personal emergencies like
this one.

"My affairs are in very good order."

"Very good," Ki had said and they had left within the
hour.

Now, Jessie turned away from her window and
prepared to meet Ki in the dining car, although she
really did not have much of an appetite. It was
mid-July and the desert heat was punishing. Long
days and nights of continuous travel had left her feeling
slightly disoriented, and she had not been sleeping or
eating particularly well.

Jessie paused by her mirror to make sure that her
appearance was not a total disaster. She studied her
reflection for a moment and noted that there were dark
shadows under her eyes. Even so, she knew she was quite

stunning. Jessie possessed a tawny mane of honey-blonde hair which glinted with a hint of copper whenever she was out in the sun. Jessie was long-legged and had high, full breasts, a slender waist, and the kind of face that caused even old men to gape and flirt like schoolboys.

"You've looked better," she said to herself as she opened her door and stepped out into the aisle to make her way toward the dining car.

"Well, well!" a big man with an enormous belly and leering eyes said as they met in the narrow aisle. "Ain't I the lucky one! I been wanting to meet and have a word alone with you, Miss Starbuck. My name is John Lugo."

Jessie had no idea how Lugo had learned her name but it was not as if she was not well-known. Anyway, she found him very repulsive. She could smell foul, reeking whiskey on Lugo's breath and she took immediate offense to the way his eyes fixed on her breasts as if he were starving and they were delicacies that he intended to devour.

"Please step aside," Jessie said, making no effort to hide either her disgust or her impatience.

"Step aside? Oh no! We got a whole lot to talk about, Miss Starbuck."

The man placed his hands on the walls of the narrow aisle and planted his feet wide apart. "I finally gotcha where I want you. I thought maybe we could get better acquainted over dinner. I run some cattle near Reno and I know you got a big ranch down in Texas. Maybe we could talk about breeding. Huh?"

"I've made previous arrangements," Jessie said tersely as Lugo guffawed over his own lewd suggestiveness.

"You mean with that funny-lookin' Chinaman?"

"He is a samurai, half Japanese and half American."

3

"Looks like your common, ordinary Celestial to me. He launder your panties?"

Jessie was out of patience. "Mr. Lugo, you had just better drop your hands and let me pass before someone gets hurt."

"Hurt?" The man was very large and maybe not quite as drunk as Jessie had initially thought. Lugo frowned. "I ain't meanin' to hurt anyone, unless you're into a little rough and tumble. Some women like it the hard way. And maybe you're one of 'em, huh, pretty lady?"

Jessie had heard more than enough. Her appetite, already waning, was totally gone now and she was in no mood to stomach this brute's advances. She supposed she could have returned to her private compartment and locked the door, but this bully would only take that as an admission of fear and fear always brought out the very worst in his type.

Jessie smiled disarmingly and then she stepped forward whipping her right knee up into the man's exposed groin. The blow was as hard as she could deliver and because the fool had taken such a vulnerable stance, Jessie knew that she had crushed his grapes when Lugo squalled and his eyes bugged with agony.

"Now," Jessie said, starting to push past the big man who was doubled over, groaning and clutching his crotch, "if you'll excuse me."

She squeezed around him but to her surprise, Lugo had the presence/of mind to grab her skirt, and he was powerful enough to yank her back. Jessie tore at his face, raking bloody furrows down the sides of both his cheeks.

"You bitch!" he howled, doubling up his fist.

Jessie saw the blow coming and was able to duck. But she fell and the brute landed heavily on top of her. When she tried to break free, Lugo tore open her blouse to expose her lush breasts. Lust replaced pain in his eyes. He clamped one hand over her mouth to stifle her cries, then his hungry mouth found her breast. Jessie always carried a pistol and now her hand reached into a hidden fold of her dress and plucked at a two-shot .45 caliber derringer.

She bit his hand and when it was retracted, she was able to cry, "Stop it!"

But he was crazy with desire so Jessie dragged the derringer out and, still not willing to kill him outright, she pressed it to his buttocks and pulled the trigger.

Lugo had been kneeling over her, one knee planted on either side of her ribs. When the bullet entered his buttocks, he jackknifed straight up and howled like a dying dog. He clamped his hand over his posterior and howled a second time as Jessie pressed her smoking derringer to his chest.

"I could have put that bullet though your belly, mister, instead of where you keep your brains. Now get off me or I'll put the next slug through your heart."

The man's chin dipped and when Lugo saw the smoking derringer shoved against his chest, his eyes widened with stark terror. He scrambled to his feet and he stared down at Jessie with such hatred that she decided that the pain might have driven him senseless.

Neither of them saw the samurai suddenly appear in the aisle. It took Ki a split second to apprise the situation and then he delivered a sweeping lotus kick to the big man's face that broke his nose and sent him flying over backward. Ki jumped over Jessie and landed on Lugo's chest. Before Jessie could even speak, she saw the samurai's hand chop downward in a knife-hand blow that caught Lugo at the base of his thick neck.

5

The man quivered into silence.

"Are you all right, Jessie?" Ki asked, pivoting around to see her drawing her torn blouse together and sitting up. "Did he hurt you?"

She was shaken and felt soiled, but was otherwise all right. "I'm fine, Ki. But at the next whistle stop, make sure that Mr. Lugo exits this train, conscious or unconscious."

"What else can I do?"

"Bring me a porter with hot water so that I can take a bath."

"And food?"

"Perhaps later in my private berth."

"I was waiting in the dining car. I'm sorry that I was not closer."

"That's all right. There was no way for you or me to anticipate that this man would get drunk enough to behave like such a beast. Maybe we taught him a lesson in manners that he will not soon forget."

"I know one thing," the samurai said, "he will not be able to walk or sit without pain for a long, long time."

"Why don't you join me in my compartment in about two hours? We can eat and talk in private before the train pulls into Reno. Perhaps you have some thoughts about Amy's letter that I need to hear."

The samurai reached over and grabbed Jessie's attacker by the boots and dragged him up the aisle which was now filling with curious passengers. Blood was flowing from the gaping hole in Lugo's torn buttocks and it was leaving an unfortunate smear that caused one woman to swoon.

"Out of the way," the samurai ordered as he dragged Jessie's now unconscious assailant out of the coach to an opening between cars where he could be disposed of in a very unceremonious fashion as soon as the train stopped.

Jessie returned to her traveling compartment and poured herself a glass of whiskey. This was not the first time that a man had completely lost his senses and tried to rape her and Jessie doubted that it would be the last. The West was filled with rough, unprincipled men, just as surely as there were those who were brave and honorable.

When she was finished with her drink, she heard a knock on her door. Then, "Porter, Miss Starbuck."

The porter brought in hot water and filled her bath. He was a wonderful fellow, an ex-slave from Georgia named Theodore Wilson.

"I's sorry for all that trouble, Miss Starbuck."

"Me too," she said. "But it's all right."

"Yo friend, he's already pitched Mr. Lugo off de train."

"He did? I don't recall us stopping."

"Well," Theodore said, "we did slow down a mite back yonder."

"Then I suppose that Mr. Lugo will have a long walk and plenty of time to consider his wretched behavior."

" 'Bout a hundred miles, Miss Starbuck."

Jessie wondered if Lugo would even survive such a journey out here in the heat of the desert. But then, she remembered that the Union Pacific eastbound would be coming through tomorrow and she would bet anything that Lugo would risk being run down attempting to stop it in order to keep from dying of thirst.

"Perhaps Mr. Lugo will go east to find a good surgeon in order to remove a .45 caliber slug from his . . . anatomy."

Wilson winked and then he chuckled because everyone on the train had heard the story and knew exactly in which part of Lugo's "anatomy" Jessie's slug could be found.

• • •

Two hours later, Ki joined Jessie in her quarters and shared a plate of cold, sliced beef and some potatoes washed down with coffee. Ki did not drink strong spirits, for he believed that they would detract from his extraordinary physical skills that he employed as a samurai and Jessie's sworn protector.

"When we reach Reno," Jessie said, "we'll take a coach down to Carson City and see Amy."

"Maybe her father and brother have shown up and we will have made this trip for nothing," the samurai said.

"I don't think so," Jessie replied. "I dispatched a telegram from Denver asking her to send me a telegram at Cheyenne and again at Elko if we were not needed. There were no telegrams at either location so I think that Amy still needs us."

"It is hard to plan when she gives us so little information."

"I know," Jessie agreed. "All I can say is that Amy Ross has always been very composed and is not the sort of person to jump to wild conclusions or to panic. That's why this letter is so troubling. Amy would not have asked for our help unless she was very, very sure that both her father and her brother were either dead, or in serious jeopardy."

Ki nodded. He knew and liked both men although it had been almost three years since he'd seen them.

"Ki?"

He looked directly into her eyes. Ki was dark, lithe and handsome. He wore a black, loose-fitting ninja costume, a braided leather headband and sandals.

"I heard," Jessie continued, "that you have already given Mr. Lugo the opportunity to witness the beauty of the desert's solitude."

"He will perhaps find wisdom in reflection," Ki said without batting an eye.

"Did the man have any water on him?"

"Personal suffering often leads to an awareness of the soul," Ki told her, informing Jessie that the man did not have any water and would, therefore, suffer thirst in addition to his other wounds and accumulated injuries.

"I don't think I've ever seen you strike anyone at the base of the neck with such force. I thought sure that you must have killed the man."

"Almost," the samurai admitted.

"I'm glad that you did not."

Ki said nothing.

"How long has it been since we were forced into this terrible desert in the middle of summer?"

"Three years," the samurai told her.

"It was when we were trying to find that missing child."

The samurai nodded. They had rescued a white child abducted by the Paiute Indians. The trail had been one fraught with dangers and suffering. But they had saved the little girl and all their suffering had been worth the effort. Jessie just hoped that this search for Amy Ross's relatives would end with the same favorable results.

★

Chapter 2

Jessie and Ki were more than ready to depart the train at Reno, Nevada. Jessie had always liked this town, founded as an emigrant crossing at the Truckee River. She knew that most of the businesses and well-tended houses that faced the tree-lined streets had not been here before the Central Pacific Railroad had auctioned lots in 1868. This was only a year before the completion of the transcontinental railroad. Now, however, Reno was a major distribution point for the Comstock Lode, Carson City and all of western Nevada.

Jessie paid a carriage driver to deliver them to the nearest stageline so they could travel on down to Carson City, some thirty miles to the south. Their driver needled his way down busy Virginia Street, over the Truckee River bridge, and on to a stageline called simply the Overland Express.

"There you go, miss," the driver said, unloading Jessie's bags and taking them up to the stage office.

"Thank you." Jessie paid the man and said, "Do you

know if they have daily stagecoaches running to Carson City?"

"Yes, they do," the driver, a tall and thin man with a full beard, replied. "But I'm afraid that they've already left for today."

"Then there isn't much point in unloading our baggage," Jessie said. "We need to get to Carson City immediately."

"Well, miss," the driver hedged. "It's three o'clock in the afternoon and I'm afraid that all the lines have either left for Carson City or else closed their offices. Most all of 'em only have morning runs."

Jessie looked to Ki. "I suppose then, we'll have to rent livery horses."

The driver scuffed the dirt with his toes. "Miss, if you and your friend are that bound and determined to get to Carson City tonight, I'd sure be willing to take you, but I'd have to charge five dollars."

"Five dollars?"

"I got five kids, miss. The mines are not doing well and business is down. Maybe I could be talked into taking you and your friend for four dollars, but . . ."

"Five dollars would be fine," Jessie said quickly. "How soon can we leave?"

"I'd like to swap horses first. This one has been working all day. What do you say about going across the street and having a bite to eat, and I'll be waiting to pick you up when you step outside?"

"That would be fine," Jessie said.

The man beamed. "My name is Anson, Bill Anson, and I appreciate your business. I can use the money and I promise that I'll try and miss as many of the potholes as I can."

"I'm sure that you will," Jessie said. "And you'll return our baggage to your carriage?"

"Right now. And don't you worry about a thing. It'll all be safe from harm. I won't take my eyes off'n it for a single minute."

"Excellent," Jessie said with a warm smile.

Ki offered Jessie his arm and they moved across the busy street with Jessie saying, "It's too late for dinner and too early for supper, but I think that we had better eat now or we'll be starved by the time we reach Carson City."

"We ought to arrive by nine o'clock," Ki said.

"We'll check into the Ormsby House and go see Amy first thing tomorrow morning."

Jessie and Ki went into the cafe and it was plain but looked clean, and she thought that it would be just fine.

"Afternoon, miss," the owner said, appearing with an apron tied around his waist. "What can I get you and the Chinaman?"

Jessie noted how Ki stiffened with the insult. The samurai said, "I'm not a Chinaman. My name is Ki. Please address me as such."

The owner was a hefty man and he had the pugnacious jaw of a fighter, but when he matched Ki's gaze, he seemed to lose any thoughts about making an issue of Ki's ancestry.

"Whatever you say, Ki."

The martial arts master relaxed and so did Jessie. She did not like trouble, but neither would she allow her companion and protector to be slighted. Not that there was anything wrong with being Chinese, it was just that Ki was very proud of his own heritage. His mother had been Japanese, of royal blood, and his father had been a

13

wild and carefree American. The pair had fallen madly in love and so Ki was conceived. Unfortunately, Ki's father had been lost at sea and his mother, ostracized because she had married a foreigner, had died of a broken heart. Ki had never really known either of his parents, but he was still fiercely proud of them.

"What'll you have to eat?"

"Something light that doesn't take too long to prepare," Jessie said, looking to Ki to see if he agreed.

"Sounds good," Ki said.

"Mostly," the owner said, "we have steak and potatoes. How about some soup and some sourdough bread fresh out of the oven? I also have some hot apple pie for dessert."

"That will be fine," Jessie said.

"All right," Ki agrèed.

As soon as the owner was gone, Jessie looked around. The place was big enough for a dozen tables and most were occupied, even though this was an in-between time for most people to eat. At the far end of the wall were two rough freighters and they were giving Ki hard looks and making snide remarks about his dress and his long hair.

"Ki, I'm afraid that there might be trouble," Jessie said. "Perhaps we should just leave. I'm not really that hungry anyway."

"No," the samurai said quietly.

The owner reappeared with bread and glasses of cold water. Jessie said to him, "I'm afraid that those two freighters over there are looking for trouble. Would you please warn them to behave themselves?"

The owner reluctantly went over to the pair and Jessie heard him ask them to simmer down and behave.

"Behave, hell!" one of them challenged. "We didn't

know that you served Chinamen in here with us white folks!"

"He's not a Chinaman, and I'm not so sure that it would matter to me even if he were. Now either mind your manners or I'm going to have to ask you boys to leave."

One of the men jerked his six-gun out and aimed it at the owner's gut. He grinned wickedly and said, "Askin' won't cut it, mister. So how are you going to *make* us leave?"

"Excuse me," Ki said, coming to his feet and moving over to the owner.

Jessie took a sip of water. She had witnessed this same sort of scene many times and could predict the outcome. Even so, she was continually amazed by the samurai and could not help but watch.

"My name is Ki," he said, bowing to the two surprised patrons. "And I believe there is some misunderstanding here?"

"No misunderstanding a'tall!" the larger of the pair said, gun still in his fist but now shifting it in Ki's direction. "We just don't like the idea of a damn Chink eating in the same damned cafe with us."

"Too bad," Ki said, almost sympathetically. "But that being the unfortunate case, I think you had both better leave and find somewhere else to eat."

"Huh?"

"You heard him," the owner said. "And I'll be damned if I don't feel the same way!"

The two freighters grinned and the bigger one said, "Yeah, but you ain't the one that's got a gun in his hand, are you?"

Several of the other patrons eased out of their chairs and started to leave before the trouble started, but Ki didn't give them the chance to reach the door. Sweeping his hand up in a *migi-shotei* blow, he brought the leather-hard edge of his hand upward so fast that it was a blur before it struck the man's wrist and sent his gun spinning across the room. The man grunted in pain and before he could push himself up from his chair, Ki delivered a *tegatana* blow that caught the big man just behind his ear and dropped him face forward into his bowl of chicken soup. The man bellowed as the hot soup burned his face and he flopped over backward.

Ki took his fighting stance and the second freighter just blinked with indecision. Ki decided to help him. "Either fight or grab your friend and run."

"But not," the owner said quickly, "before they pay their bill."

"That's right," Ki said. "Fight, or pay up and get out."

"I'm payin', I'm payin'," the freighter said, yanking out a wad of greenbacks and acting so frightened that he did not even bother to count them out.

In a moment, they were gone.

"All right," the owner said, "the show is over and there is more coffee coming up for anyone that wants it. We got apple pie for dessert, and it's only two bits. You all better speak up before it's all claimed."

The other patrons were quick to order as Ki returned to his seat. The owner came over and said, "I never saw anyone fight like that. Where the deuce did you learn to throw them chops and punches?"

"It's a long story and I'm afraid Ki does not have time to explain," Jessie said. "Could we have more sourdough bread right away?"

"You betcha!" the owner said, dashing into the kitchen and yelling back over his shoulder. "And I'm going to

16

make sure that you both get a free slice of Edna's apple pie!"

Jessie had no idea who Edna was but she had a feeling that the pie was going to be excellent.

"That Edna sure makes good pie," the driver said when Ki and Jessie exited the cafe. "I should have told you to order some. Especially the apple."

"We had some," Jessie said, "and it was wonderful."

"Best pie in Nevada," Anson bragged.

The driver had substituted a sprightly dapple-gray mare for the weary bay gelding. She had a flaxen tail and mane and moved south out of Reno at a smart pace.

"Nice mare," Jessie said.

"You bet she is! I knew you were in sort of a hurry and I was afraid that my gelding, being old and tired, would have just plodded along. But this mare, she just plain likes to travel."

"Is she also a good saddle horse?" Jessie asked.

"They don't come any better. I paid thirty dollars for her and she's worth twice as much. Only five years old and her gait is so smooth that it will rock you to sleep. She's as sound as a dollar and a good keeper."

"I can see that," Jessie said. "Would you be interested in selling her?"

Anson looked over at Jessie. "Everything I got except my family is for sale, if'n I hear the right price."

"And what is the right price?"

"Have to have at least fifty dollars for her."

"After I see about my friend Amy," Jessie said, "I might just be willing to pay your price."

"You would?"

"She is an outstanding mare," Jessie said. "I just don't know if I'll be needing a horse. I'll find out tomorrow morning. So if you want to hold over tonight and come around about noon, I'll have an answer for you."

"Fifty dollars is more than I can make in two months of driving people around town. Why, sure I'll wait!"

The rest of the trip down to Carson City was quite pleasant. Jessie had always enjoyed the magnificent scenery that unfolded between Reno and Carson City. It was also quite varied. Just south of town lay a field of sulphur hot springs that smoked and bubbled. Miners from the Comstock Lode swore that it was a tonic to bathe in the sulfur springs, if you didn't pick the wrong one and get boiled. To the east you could clearly see the road leading up to famed Virginia City and the Comstock Lode. That was just below Sun Mountain and farther on, Slide Mountain and Mount Rose were adorned with snow, even this late in the year.

Perhaps most beautiful of all was the lovely Washoe Valley with its shallow but picturesque lake surrounded by rich grassland. They traveled up the timbered Franktown Road and finally, just at sunset, they topped a grade and there before them stretched Carson City, the state's capital.

"Looks as if it's grown a little," Ki said.

"It's doin' right fine," Anson said. "I've got applications in to work for the state."

"Doing what?" Jessie asked.

"Building roads, most likely. But I'd take most anything. State offers steady work and steady pay."

"That's a real benefit to a man with five children."

"Sure is, miss! Them little beggars eat, whether there is work or not."

Jessie liked this man. He drove them smartly down the long grade into Carson City as the sun was dying and glittering off the great domed capitol building. At the Ormsby House, the driver pulled the mare in and helped them unload their baggage and tote it into the lobby.

"I'll be back around noon tomorrow to see if you still want to buy my mare," Anson said. "Is there anything I can do for you before I leave?"

Bill Anson looked very tired and Jessie supposed the poor man had been working since early morning. "No, get some rest. We'll see you tomorrow about the horse."

"You'd sure like her under a saddle, miss. I call her Lady and that's what you strike me as."

"Thank you," Jessie said, paying the man an extra dollar tip. "And good night."

The Ormsby House was quite familiar to Jessie and Ki, and the hotel desk clerk was delighted to see them again.

"Hello, Bob," Jessie said, shaking the clerk's hand. "I sure hope that you have a couple of rooms for Ki and myself at this late hour."

"If I didn't," Bob said, "we'd evict our guests to make room for you both."

When Jessie raised her eyebrows, Bob quickly added, "Only kidding, Miss Starbuck. We do have a couple of rooms still empty and we're delighted that you have come again to be our guests."

Jessie and Ki were shown to their rooms. Jessie was so tired that she did not even think about eating a late supper and bid good night to the samurai and went straight to bed.

In the middle of the night, she awakened to the sound of shouting and gunfire. Tiptoeing to her window, she saw the cause to be a couple of drunks who were looking to get jailed for disturbing the peace. And sure enough, a marshal appeared, hurrying along on foot. Jessie saw him disarm one of the celebrants and be forced to pistol-whip the other. Then the marshal grabbed each one by an ankle and dragged them slowly off to jail,

"Nice town," Jessie said. "And nice work, Marshal."

When she returned to bed, Jessie found sleep difficult. She was very worried about Amy but glad that tomorrow she would finally discover the true gravity of the situation that affected her dear old friend. And what if Amy's father and brother had suddenly been found and this was merely a false alarm?

So much the better, Jessie thought. Because then we'll just sightsee and go up and enjoy the cool mountains at Lake Tahoe for a week or two.

★

Chapter 3

The stately, two-story Ross home was located three blocks west of the main street on Kings Canyon Road. When Ki and Jessie arrived, the house looked empty and it was tightly shuttered, but they mounted the porch steps and knocked loudly anyway.

"It appears that Amy isn't home," Jessie said, not able to hide her disappointment.

"What shall we do?" Ki asked.

"There isn't much that we can do except come back in a few hours and hope that she returns," Jessie said.

"Yoo-hoo! Oh, yoo-hoo!"

Both Ki and Jessie turned to see a very heavyset woman standing on her front porch. She was clutching a small, yapping dog and both the woman and her pet were quite obviously excited.

"Maybe she can tell us something about Amy," Jessie said, leaving the porch and heading across the yard.

Ki followed and when they stood at the base of the woman's steps, they tried to carry on a conversation, but the dog was barking so furiously that the heavyset woman finally just opened her door and tossed him inside, then slammed the door shut.

"Hercules just drives me crazy sometimes!" the woman exclaimed. "I don't know why he's so excitable!"

"I'm sure he isn't like that all the time," Jessie said, trying to think of something nice to say about the dog which was still frantically barking.

"Well, he *is* a real cutie, isn't he," the woman said, digging a handkerchief out of her shapeless housedress and wiping sweat from her brow and neck.

"Were you trying to tell us something?" Jessie asked. "Perhaps something about Miss Ross?"

"Are you Miss Starbuck?"

"I am, and this is my friend, Ki."

The woman cocked her head a little sideways, like a bird studying a morsel of food. She would far outweigh Ki and she looked a bit predatory to Jessie.

"My, my, he's a handsome one, isn't he!" the fat woman said, dabbing at her glistening cleavage.

"Yes," Jessie said, "and he speaks English, too. Now, what is it that I need to know about Amy?"

"Well," the woman said, "would you like to come inside and have some lemonade? It is getting warm out."

"I'm sorry," Jessie replied, "but we are in a bit of a hurry. Perhaps another time. Now, about Amy?"

"Oh that poor dear!" the woman exclaimed. "The marshal came two days ago to tell Miss Ross that they had found her father and he'd been murdered! Can you imagine!"

Jessie took a deep breath and expelled it slowly. "Where?"

The woman blinked. "Why, I forget. But I saw Miss Ross leaving in a hurry and I'm sure that she has gone off to claim her poor father's body, or what remains of it."

"Any news of her missing brother?" Ki asked.

"Oh," the woman cooed, "you *do* have a tongue, you sly rogue, you!"

Jessie saw Ki's cheeks color, perhaps with embarrassment, but more likely with exasperation. "Miss . . . ," Jessie began.

"Miss Applethorpe. Constance Applethorpe."

"Yes, Miss Applethorpe. Since you knew my name, Amy must have left some message that was to be passed on to us when we arrived."

"She said to tell you that she would return with her father's body and the burial would be here in Carson City. And that you were both to stay at her home and wait."

Jessie did not find that idea at all appealing. "Are you certain that you can't remember where her father's body was discovered?"

"No," the woman said, wrinkling her brow and mopping her glistening face again. "But I'm positive that Marshal Fetterman could tell you."

"Thank you," Jessie said. "We'll go see the marshal right now."

"You know," the woman said coming down from the porch and following them out to the street, "the rumor is that Miss Ross's father and brother struck it rich somewhere out in the middle of Nevada."

"Did you ever see any sign of that wealth coming to Amy?" Jessie asked.

"No, she was a dear girl and she worked for the

legislature when it was in session. Her father, you understand, was once a successful merchant here in town and he had quite a lot of money saved up. I'm sure that he must have gone a little crazy to have sold his prosperous store and then gone prospecting."

"Well," Jessie said, "I knew the man and it was his dream to strike it rich."

"Both the father and his son probably got snuffed for their gold," the woman said, shaking her sagging chins. "There's some awful crazy people running around out there in the hills. And don't forget the Indians. Some people think that we've whipped them, but they're sneaky and they'll still scalp a white man whenever they get the chance."

Jessie had heard about enough. The Paiutes had been subjugated a decade earlier and they were now a very docile and poor tribe living on government reservations. But Jessie knew that explaining these facts to the woman was not going to make a bit of difference in her attitude.

"You come back for that lemonade whenever you want!" the woman called as Jessie and Ki started back for town.

"That'll be the day," Ki muttered under his breath.

"I'm sorry to hear that we are too late to help Amy's father," Jessie said, "and it doesn't look good for Ken, either."

Ken Ross was about their age, a tall, somewhat quiet young man who had idolized his father and had once gone east to a medical school but who had returned within a year because he could not stand to be long away from the openness of the great American West.

"Ken is tough," Ki said. "And not just physically. If he were caught by surprise, he would do everything in his power to escape."

"I know that," Jessie said. "But I also know that he would never have abandoned his father. No, my sad conclusion is that, if Amy's father is dead, so is her brother."

"Maybe," Ki said, "the marshal can give us enough details to piece the whole thing together."

Marshal Amos O. Fetterman was a large man with twenty years of experience and the scars to prove it. He had grown up in Iowa as a farmboy but had come west when he was eighteen and had fought during the Paiute War. He'd gone over the Sierra Nevada Mountains but hadn't found much in the way of gold because all the placer ore had long since been mined out. With the momentous discovery of the huge Comstock Lode, Fetterman had tried his hand at mining, for the wages were high. But he'd discovered he was claustrophobic and, after being a teamster for several years, had drifted into the law profession.

"Miss Starbuck!" Fetterman said. "I've been expecting you and your friend. Come on in and pull up a chair."

Jessie shook her head. "We just learned that Mr. Ross was murdered and that Amy has gone to claim his body."

"There wasn't much left to claim, I'm afraid. Would you care to pull up a chair? You and Ki look as if you've had better mornings."

"That's for certain," Jessie said. She patted her blouse pocket. "We've come all the way from Texas to help Amy, but it appears that we are much too late."

"You're too late to save her father, but maybe not her brother, Ken."

"Then he is alive."

"I didn't say that," Fetterman murmured. "I just said

25

that the authorities over in Eureka hadn't found any trace of his body. But, Miss Starbuck, as you may or may not know, that region is riddled with old mine shafts and someone could throw a body down one and it would never be found."

"I see." Jessie took a deep breath. "How was Amy taking all of this?"

"Very hard, as you might well expect. But she was trying to be calm and brave and her brother means a great deal to her. Amy left Carson City the day before yesterday. I expect that she still hasn't arrived in Eureka."

"I wish she would have waited for us," Ki said.

"We talked about it but she couldn't be sure when you'd arrive. And put yourself in her place. Would you have waited if your father's corpse was waiting in some distant mining town?"

"No," Jessie said tightly, "of course not. Is there a stagecoach that is leaving for Eureka today?"

"I'm afraid that Amy caught the weekly supply coach."

"Then we'll have to buy horses and outfits and go ourselves," Jessie said.

"Do you really think that there is much point?" the marshal asked. "I mean, the damage is already done."

"Maybe we can help to find Ken."

"I'd like to offer you some encouragement about that," Marshal Fetterman said, "but I can't. Ken and his father were mighty close and one could always be found near the other. I'm telling you, Miss Starbuck, if Amy's father was murdered, then so was her brother."

"Thank you for your time," Jessie said, not wanting to hear any more of this man's theories. "But, like Amy, that's something that we'll just have to find out for ourselves."

"I can give you the name of a man who has good horses for sale."

"I've already one in mind," Jessie said, "but Ki will need a sound horse that can travel fast."

"The fella's name is Quinn."

"First name or last?"

"I honestly don't know," the marshal said. "Quinn runs a livery at the south end of town and you need to tell him that I sent you over. That way at least he won't try and snooker you too bad on the price."

"We'll do that," Jessie said, starting for the door, where she stopped and turned to look back. "Marshal, do you think that they really did find a big gold strike out there someplace in the middle of Nevada?"

"I do," the marshal said without a moment's hesitation. "Old George Ross was one of the sharpest characters that I ever come across. He'd made his fortune in dry goods, but he had gotten a taste of gold fever when he went to California, same as me back in 1850. Once you get bit by the bug, you never completely recover. Anyway, George wrote Amy about the discovery. She told me about the letter and said that it was supposed to be worth a fortune. Now, George would never have lied to Amy and he wasn't the kind of man that would make a mistake and get all excited about something like fool's gold."

"I agree," Jessie said. "If George said he'd discovered a fortune, then he did."

"Well," the marshal said, "there must've been some others that caught wind of that letter. I told Amy never to tell anyone about her father and brother's discovery, but she probably told a few of her friends who told a few of their friends. All I know is that the discovery wasn't a secret for very long. There was even an article about it in the damned newspaper!"

"And that would attract buzzards to the bait," Jessie said. "What a pity that George Ross didn't even have a chance to enjoy the fruits of his labor."

"Yeah," the marshal said. "Amy didn't come right out and say it, but from what I read between the lines, her father had been dead for a good many weeks before they discovered what was left of his body. It was discovered down one of those deep shafts that I told you about and it's a wonder that it was recovered at all."

"Amy must have taken that pretty hard," Jessie said.

"She about went crazy," the marshal admitted. "We finally got her calmed down, but she couldn't bear staying in Carson City until you and Ki arrived to accompany her to Eureka."

"We'll catch up with her," Ki vowed. "Perhaps even before she reaches her father's remains."

"I hope that someone figures out who killed George. If I wasn't nailed down to this desk and paid for by the people of this fair city, I'd go off and investigate the murder myself."

"I'm sure that you would," Jessie said as she passed on out the door.

★
Chapter 4

Quinn was a tall, heavyset man who chewed on the stub of an unlit cigar and liked to stare at pretty women. When he saw Jessie coming into his livery, the cigar stub dropped forgotten to the dirt and he hissed, "Holy shit!"

But not loud enough for Jessie to hear.

"Afternoon, miss!" he called out, showing his big tobacco-stained teeth. "Fine morning to go for a buggy ride."

"Marshal Fetterman said that you sold good horses at a reasonable price."

Quinn sized Jessie up as not only stunning, but also well-to-do. "Why, that was real nice of the marshal to pay me that there little compliment. And yes, I do sell far too cheap, but I like helpin' people. Makin' you happy just naturally makes me happy, miss."

The samurai rolled his eyes and even Jessie thought that Quinn was laying it on excessively thick. She said, "I've already got a horse but my friend Ki needs a good mount."

"Oh," Quinn said, looking disappointed. "I was hopin' that I might be able to interest you in a fine saddle mare."

"Nope. What have you got that Ki can ride?"

Quinn sized the samurai up without much enthusiasm. "From the looks of him, I'd say he needs something pretty damned tame, miss. To be honest, he don't exactly look like a regular hand, now does he?"

"I'm a good horseman," Ki said. "Despite what you might think. And I won't be cheated or given a poor animal."

"Oh you won't, will you?" Quinn said, cocking an eyebrow. "Well, I . . . sure. Whatever you say. Customer is always right, at least that's what old George Ross used to remind me. And it worked for him."

"George was right," Jessie said. "Now what do you have for my friend?"

"Come on over to this stall and have a peek," Quinn said, motioning them both over to the right until they were able to peer inside a stall at a handsome pinto.

Quinn let them admire the horse for several moments, then he said, "That there horse is the finest animal in western Nevada, bar none. Maybe there's a few faster, but I doubt it. And sound! Lordy, is he sound! He's a real tough critter with the wind to carry you wherever you want in a mighty big hurry."

Jessie opened the stall and stepped inside. She ran her hands up and down the pinto's legs, checking to see if he had wind splints or any bone problems. She found none and checked the hooves one at a time. A horse with bad feet was no good at all, especially in the rough country of Central Nevada.

"He needs to be shod," Jessie said.

"Oh," Quinn replied, "I suspect we can work up a deal

30

that would include a fresh pair of shoes. Just so happens, I shoe horses and I've never had any complaints about my work."

"How much?" Jessie asked, coming right to the issue.

"Have to have a hundred dollars." Seeing Jessie's surprise and disapproval, he quickly added, "Of course, that would include a saddle."

"I'll need two saddles and bridles and, if they're top notch, I'll give you fifty dollars for everything."

"For that pinto, two saddles and bridles, and I suppose you'd want horse blankets thrown in."

"Good ones," Jessie said.

Quinn found another stump of a cigar in his pocket and jammed it into his mouth. "Let's see, miss, I'd have to have . . . oh, I suppose I could let you have all that for about seventy dollars, but I'd be skinnin' myself. I truly would."

"No, you wouldn't," Ki said. "I'll bet you didn't pay over thirty dollars for the pinto and you can buy used saddles all day long for ten dollars each. So you'd be making a nice profit."

"Unless you are a part of this transaction, mister, I'll thank you not to muddy the waters."

Thus rebuked, Ki stepped over to the pinto and scratched his neck. Ki was a good horseman but not of the caliber of Jessie, who had practically been born and reared on a horse.

"Seventy-five dollars for two saddles, two bridles and blankets and this pinto gets four new shoes. It's a deal."

"It's a bad deal," Quinn said. "I'm killin' myself with kindness for my fellow man . . . in your case woman."

"I think you'll live for quite a while longer," Jessie said. "We'll be back in a half hour to pick up the horse."

"I can't even fire my forge and tack the shoes on that fast!"

"All right," Jessie said, "we'll give you a full hour. But after that, we're leaving."

"What's your big, all-fired hurry?"

"We're going to Eureka to help Amy Ross find out what happened to her father and brother."

"Old George Ross was killed."

"We know that," Jessie said, "but Ken Ross is still missing."

"That's because the people at Eureka still ain't checked all the mine shafts for bodies. And I suspect, if they do, Ken's body will be found along with a few others that either got too drunk or made bad enemies."

"Either way," Jessie replied, "we need to catch up to that stage that is carrying Amy and then see what we can do to help her."

"That's a good sentiment," Quinn acknowledged as he haltered the pinto and led him out of his stall. "I sure do hate to give this horse away, though."

"Throw in a couple of canteens, halters and lead ropes . . . and a sack of grain tied across the back of the saddle . . . and I'll pay you ninety dollars."

Quinn grinned. "Now you're talking! Sure enough, I'll have this fine animal ready in one hour. But ridin' all the way to Eureka ain't going to bring back George Ross. He's a goner and so is his son."

"Maybe, but maybe not," Jessie said on her way out the door.

Bill Anson was waiting with the dapple-gray mare when Jessie and Ki returned to the Ormsby House to claim their belongings.

"I know that you'll take good care of Lady," Anson

said, scratching the mare's neck. "She's a fine animal and she'll never give you a hint of trouble."

"I'm sure that is true," Jessie said, noting Anson's regret to part with the beautiful animal.

"If you'll take her over to Mr. Quinn's stable, he'll saddle her and ask him to check her shoes."

"They're almost new," Anson said. "You don't have to worry about that."

"Good." Jessie paid the man and then turned to leave. "And by the way, thanks for bringing us to Carson City."

"Thanks for hiring me."

"Have you got a way to get you and your carriage back to Carson City?"

"I'll buy a horse from Quinn," the man said. "It won't be near the quality of that gray mare, but he's got some sound horses and he's always treated me pretty fairly."

"Good," Jessie said.

When Jessie and Ki left, they went to a mercantile to purchase supplies for their long trip to Eureka. Jessie knew that the mining town was at least two hundred miles to the east. Two hundred miles of scorching desert, sun-blasted mountains and damn little water.

"You'll have a hard, hard ride," the owner of the mercantile warned. "You'd better take plenty of water and ammunition."

"Why ammunition?" Ki asked.

"There's been a flurry of hold-ups and murders on that trail through Austin and on to Eureka. Some say it's Indians, but I think it's just white men that turned bad when the mines started layin' off their work force."

"Either way, they're outlaws," Jessie said.

"You bet they are and they mean business. Several people who resisted have been shot. My advice, if they jump you, is just to give them whatever they want. Better your money than your lives, don't you agree?"

"No," Ki said flatly. "When you start to give in to lawlessness, it's the beginning of the end."

"Well," the man said, "I guess if they was to jump out in front of you from behind a rock, real sudden like, you'd have damn little choice but to do what they demanded."

"You don't know us," Jessie said. "We are not of a mind to cave in to the demands of highwaymen."

"Suit yourself," the man said. "I was just trying to offer you some good advice."

Ki picked up their purchases which had been stuffed into a burlap bag and turned his back on the man. He would tie everything behind his saddle and he would keep his eyes open for trouble on the road to Eureka.

Jessie and Ki went back to Quinn's to pick up their horses and supplies.

Marshal Amos Fetterman was waiting to see them off. When Jessie and Ki were mounted, he stepped up to Jessie and said, "You just be real careful out there, miss. It's rough and lawless country. If there was some way that I could go with you and your friend, I would. But I can't."

"We understand," Jessie said. "And we're prepared to meet whatever troubles might befall us along the way."

Fetterman nodded, but the worry lines in his face did not soften. Jessie couldn't help that. All she could do was to get to Eureka as fast as possible and try to help poor Amy Ross.

"Let's ride," she said to Ki. "We got a long ways to go."

The samurai nodded and they galloped out of town. It was high noon and already hotter than the fires of hell.

★

Chapter 5

Amy Ross simply could not believe that her stagecoach was being held up by a trio of highwaymen. Here they were, just two days out of Carson City and struggling to get over the high, rugged Shoshone Mountains, and they were about to be robbed! Amy had just about had enough of lawlessness. She was still devastated and angry over the death of her poor father who had never hurt anyone, and also the disappearance of her brother, and now here were these damned highwaymen.

"Miss, what are you doing?" the heavyset and middle-aged man across the seat from her demanded, his eyes widening with alarm. "You . . . you aren't thinking of using that gun, are you?"

"I am and I will!" Amy said convincingly as she dragged an old Colt .45 out of her satchel.

Delbert Denton shook his head, jowls shaking. "Please, Miss Ross! You'll only succeed in getting us all killed if you resist these men. We'll just do as they say and hope they are merciful."

"Not on your life, Mr. Denton!" Amy cocked the hammer of the pistol and held it tightly in both hands. "My father and brother both taught me how to shoot and hit what I aim for at a very young age. And they taught me to fight for what is mine."

"But they might kill us both!"

Amy peered out the window. The three highwaymen had stopped the coach on a steep climb and now they were ordering the driver and his shotgun guard to throw away their weapons and climb down from the coach.

"Dammit!" Amy swore. "I can't see them well enough to get a clean shot!"

"Please! Don't cause any . . ."

Denton's words were interrupted as two gunshots shattered the thin mountain air. Amy saw the driver pitch over the side of the coach and land facedown on the road with a sickening crunch. He didn't even quiver.

"They shot him down in cold blood!" Denton squealed. "My God, now they're going to kill us for sure!"

Amy knew that Denton was right, especially when she heard three more shots and then recognized the unmistakable sound of the guard's body striking the hard road and the poor man's neck snapping like a dry branch.

"Mr. Denton," she whispered, "if you've got a weapon, you'd better drag it out and be prepared to use it because these men are not merciful."

Amy tried to swallow her fear but her throat was too dry. The gun in her hands was shaking as if it were a live thing and she very much doubted that she could hit anything if she did not calm down. She watched as Denton found a worthless little derringer in his traveling bag.

36

"That's the best you've got?" Amy asked, trying but failing to hide her disappointment.

"It is," Denton said, his round face shining with perspiration. "But I assure you, Miss Ross, I will use it against anyone who tries to hurt me . . . or you."

Denton's brave declaration surprised Amy and gave her a measure of badly needed hope. "I expect we had just better let them come to us."

Denton nodded. "Excellent idea. But I think we ought to warn them that we are armed. If we do that, perhaps they will decide to go away."

"Uh-uh," Amy said. "They would just ride off a ways and start shooting the coach up. They'd riddle it with bullets and we wouldn't have a chance."

"Then what . . ."

"When they come to open the door, we open fire," Amy said, anticipating Denton's question.

Amy was afraid to stick her head out the window so she stayed in the middle of the coach because its interior was cloaked in deep shadow. She could hear the highwaymen talking excitedly and then she felt the coach move as one of them climbed up to see if it was carrying a strongbox.

"Ain't nothing here!"

"Get the passengers out," a man growled. "They're always good for a few dollars and some jewelry."

A horseman appeared in view. He was tall and thin with a hooked nose and a scraggly, black handlebar mustache. He looked dirty and Amy only had to take one quick look at the man to realize that there wasn't a hint of mercy on his hawkish face. She watched him level his gun at the window. The muzzle of his six-shooter looked as big as that of a cannon. Amy dropped flat on the seat.

"Get down, Mr. Denton!" she hissed. "They're going to open fire on the coach."

Denton wasn't about to play the hero. With a cry of alarm, he pitched over and burrowed up hard against the floor.

"Any passengers inside had better get their asses out of that coach and come out with their hands in the air!" the horseman ordered. "And I mean right gawddamn now!"

"What are we going to do!" Denton wheezed, breathing so hard that you would have thought he'd run ten miles.

"They've killed the driver and guard and they're not wearing masks," Amy said in a voice so tight with fear that she hardly recognized it as her own. "They're going to rob and then kill us, Mr. Denton. We've got to kill them first."

"They may keep you alive," Denton said, without really thinking. "They'll probably want to toy with you for their lustful pleasures."

"They'll have to kill me first," Amy heard herself say as she took a deep breath and tried to calm her nerves. "Mr. Denton, are you ready?"

He was so frightened that Amy was afraid the poor man was going to faint and be of no help at all. Amy jumped up, took a split second aim and fired at the cruel-looking horseman. She had the satisfaction of seeing the horseman take her bullet squarely in the chest. The man jerked back in his saddle, his chin dropped and he stared at the red rose that was spreading on his filthy white shirt. He looked up at Amy and he blinked. His jaw dropped open in amazement and then he pitched forward over the front of his horse.

All hell broke loose after that.

Out of the corner of her eye, Amy saw another horseman spurring into view and she fired, but missed. Two bullets splintered through the side of the coach and she heard Denton grunt with pain, then hit the floorboards.

"Mr. Denton!"

He was dead, shot through the forehead. Amy cried out in fury and raised up just in time to see another rider appear on the other side of the coach. He couldn't see her clearly, but she had a good view of him and she opened fire, drilling him in the neck. Amy saw his face turn pale as he grabbed his neck while his horse raced away. Amy knew that the man would bleed to death very quickly.

"One more," Amy choked, turning to glance at Denton. "And I'm going to get him too!"

But the last horseman was the smartest. He did exactly what Amy had predicted and that was to ride out of pistol range and dismount with his Winchester.

Amy peered over the lip of the window. She watched helplessly as the last highwayman levered a shell into his rifle, took aim and fired. The highwayman had all the odds in his favor. Armed with a rifle, he could take his time and pepper the coach until he either ran out of ammunition or there was no possibility that anyone inside the coach could still be alive.

"I have to get out," she said to herself. "I have to get out and run for cover."

Another bullet crashed through the side of the coach and the slug struck Denton's corpulent body.

"I'm going to shoot you to gawddamn pieces!" the rifleman screamed. "I hope I kill you slow!"

Another bullet punched through the side of the door and a splinter buried itself in Amy's forearm, causing her to cry out with pain. She removed the derringer from poor Mr. Denton's grip and then crawled over his body, grasping the side door handle. Wrenching the door open, Amy knew she dared not fall to the road or she would be seen and very likely killed before she could run for cover.

Another bullet exploded through the side of the coach and Amy flung the door open and somehow crawled over Mr. Denton. Grabbing the door, Amy hoisted herself outside and clung to the side of the coach. She was suspended just a few feet above and behind the dead shotgun guard and his weapon was lying almost within reach. Amy was tempted to jump down and snatch it up, but she knew that would be a fatal mistake because the shotgun was no match for a rifle at the range between herself and her last enemy.

"The brake," she whispered, suddenly realizing why their team of horses had not bolted in fear. No doubt, the driver had set the brake. If she could reach it without being killed, the horses would be free to run and they would carry her and the coach down the road, perhaps to a terrible death on some sharp curve, but possibly to safety.

Amy knew that there was no other choice if she were to survive. So she jumped out of the coach, lost her balance, fell and then jumped up and threw herself up toward the driver's seat and the brake. With a tremendous effort, she loosened the brake.

The horses bolted just as she had known they would. Free to escape the smell of blood and gunsmoke, they leapt forward almost spilling Amy from the coach. It was a quarter of a mile to the crest of the summit they'd been climbing and the horses took it at a run. And once over the crest, gravity drove the team on, threatening to crush them with the weight of the Concord.

The rifleman was incensed with anger. He opened fire, his slugs chasing them down the dusty road as he shouted vile curses and threats.

"Gawdamn you! I'll get you!"

Amy dragged herself up onto the driver's seat and clung to it like a wounded sparrow might cling to its perch. The horses were running as hard as they could. The lines were dragging and the coach was hurtling forward, completely out of control. Amy didn't know what would happen next and she was glad that she didn't have the time to even think about it.

She heard what sounded like a rifle banging and was sure that she was about to be shot. But then she twisted around and realized that the sound was caused by the stagecoach door that she had used to effect her escape, smashing open and shut. She clung to the seat and prayed. If the road ran for a mile or two without a sharp turn, then she just might survive. But if not . . .

The coach was gathering momentum and Amy watched as the four horses started to tire. She could see them trying to run and, at the same time, hold back the huge weight that propelled them down the steep grade. Amy grabbed the brake handle and leaned back until wood smoked and she finally felt the heavy stagecoach begin to slow.

But not soon enough. Just up ahead, she saw the road curve around the side of a mountain. Even the horses seemed to realize that they were doomed if they did not stop. One of them actually did try to squat down on his haunches and arrest the momentum of the coach, but he lost his footing and was dragged down.

"No!" Amy cried in horror as the animal began to roll

and entangle himself in the flying legs of the other horses and also drag them down.

What happened next was a blur. The coach ran over the falling horse and went airborne. Amy felt herself being lifted into the sky and she lost consciousness for a moment as she was launched over the steep mountainside.

After that, everything went blank. Amy thought that she heard the terrified screams of horses, but she could not be certain. All she knew for sure was that she struck the ground and kept rolling. It seemed that the entire world was tumbling over and over and she was spinning down a deep, dark hole into oblivion.

★

Chapter 6

Amy awoke in darkness and she might have thought she'd died except that she heard the sound of loud snoring. When she tried to sit bolt upright, a sharp pain in her side caused her to cry out.

"All right, all right," a sleepy voice said a few moments before a match flared and a lantern filled the interior of a cabin with light.

"Who are you?" Amy breathed, hands fumbling for her gun, or something else with which to defend herself.

The young man was dressed in a pair of red woolen long underwear. He had tousled brown hair, blue eyes and looked to be in his early twenties, large-boned and wide of mouth.

"Who are you?" he asked. "Since this is my cabin and claim, I get to ask the first question."

Amy took a deep breath. She squinted at the man who was regarding her with obvious curiosity. "You aren't the one with the rifle that tried to finish me off, are you?"

"No. I saw him, though. And he saw me. Fortunately, I have a rifle of my own and I am not entirely a bad shot. So we exchanged a few pleasantries and bullets, then each went our separate ways."

"But he saw me?"

"Yes, definitely."

"That means he might try and kill us both," Amy decided out loud. "He really has to kill me because I can identify him as one of the gang that tried to hold up our stage. There were two others and they gunned down both the guard and the driver."

"I suspected as much. My name is Dan. Dan Smith."

Amy nodded. "I'm Amy Ross."

His eyebrows shot up. "Are you George Ross's daughter?"

"That's right. Did you know my father?"

"Everyone knew him. I'd heard that they found him dead."

"He was murdered for gold," Amy said. "And my brother is missing."

Tears filled her eyes. "I'm afraid that Ken was also murdered and his body pitched down some deep mine shaft."

"Would you like something to eat, or drink?"

"Water."

"Good, 'cause that's about all I have," Dan said. "Other than the strongest coffee you ever saw corrode the inside of a tin pot."

Dan got up and found Amy a cup of water. She drank it down and waited until he'd returned to his own bed. In the meantime, she had the opportunity to survey her surroundings. Amy saw that the cabin was only about twelve or fifteen foot square but that it did have a stone fireplace. Winters in Central Nevada's high country could get very cold and snow was not uncommon.

"So," Dan said, "you were on your way to find out what happened to your father and brother?"

"That's right. I'd hoped that the authorities in Eureka would . . ."

"They won't help you," Dan said with assurance. "They had a marshal but he was gunned down last week. Eureka is now as lawless as Austin. There are always a few good people, though, who will try to help."

"Are you one of them?"

Dan snorted and shook his head. "I'm not the kind to leave someone who needs my help, but I'm not one to get involved in other folks' problems, either."

"Maybe you won't have any choice if that last highwayman returns to kill off the only witnesses who can really identify him."

Dan ran his fingers through his thick, curly hair. "If I ever see that man again," he said, "you can be sure that I'll shoot first and ask questions later. But for now, my main concern is your health. Did you know that you have a cracked rib?"

"No."

"Well, you do. I examined . . ."

"You *examined* me?"

"Sure! You were unconscious and in pretty bad shape when I found you. Do you remember anything about the stagecoach wreck?"

"Not much." Amy told him what she did remember but her mind was whirling and she could not quite reconcile herself to the idea that this stranger had actually *examined* her. Still, she had to admit that he'd probably saved her life, and she supposed that entitled him to a few liberties. In truth, other men had seen her body. Not many, but a few, and so it wasn't like she was a virgin, or anything.

45

When she finished telling Dan about the robbery, he shook his head. "I'm sure that someone has found the driver's and the guard's bodies by now. That road is well traveled."

"I need to reach Eureka."

"And you will," Dan promised. "Just as soon as I finish working a vein of quartz that I'm hoping will lead me to another vein of pure gold."

"But I can't wait for that!"

"It won't be long," Dan assured her. "Besides, you're certainly in no shape to travel. And anyway, I expect that there will be a search party sent out from Austin or even from Carson City. They'll probably show up here in a week or so."

"A week or so!" Amy wailed. "And what am I supposed to do until then?"

"Keep me company. Bring me good luck." Dan shrugged his shoulders. "I don't know. What do damsels in distress usually do for their rescuers?"

Amy sank back on her cot. In truth, she knew she was being a little unreasonable. Dan saved her from certain death. He had risked his own life and was still in risk of being shot for becoming involved.

"I'll wait until help comes for me," she said. "Did you know my brother, Ken?"

"Yeah," Dan said, "I knew him. We got into a fistfight about two years ago. I whipped him and he hated my guts."

Amy stared. "You fought my brother?"

"That's right."

"But why?"

"Over a girl. Not one as pretty as you, though. She was just some little dance hall girl that we'd both taken a shine to. I guess, we got a little drunk one night and the

46

next thing I knew, we were standing in the street trading punches. Your brother was tough."

"But you must have been tougher."

"I wasn't as drunk as Ken Ross. The difference between us was that, every third or fourth swing, I'd actually *land* a punch."

"Oh."

There was a long silence before Dan flopped back down on his bed and blew out the lantern. "Try to go back to sleep, Miss Ross."

"Amy," she corrected, "my name is Amy."

"Well, try to go back to sleep anyway," he said. "You're going to be real sore for a few days. I think it's a miracle that you are alive. Amy, were there any other passengers on your stagecoach?"

"One. He died instantly."

There was a long silence and then Dan said, "That fella that tried to kill us after I got to the wreck first, he was a little crazy, wasn't he."

"What do you mean?"

"He was shouting and screaming. I never saw anything like him. I expect that was one of the reasons why his aim was so bad."

"My aim wasn't bad," Amy said after a few moments. "I killed that man's two friends. I never killed anyone before, but I'd do it again, given the chance."

"You're a tough woman," Dan said. "Tough and pretty. That's a rare combination."

"Is it?"

"You bet! Whores are tough, but they're usually harder than iron inside and few of them are pretty."

"Except for the one that you and my brother fought over."

"Yes," Dan said after a few moments. "Except for her."

Amy felt tears on her cheeks. "Did you know that my father and brother struck it rich somewhere over by Eureka?"

"Do tell?"

"That's why they were killed."

"You said 'they.' I guess you've come to the conclusion that your brother really is dead."

"If Ken were alive, he'd have surfaced and then demanded justice for our father."

"Maybe," Dan said, "the same men that killed your father have taken your brother hostage and intend to make him tell them where they struck it rich."

"I don't think so," Amy said, shaking her head in the darkness. "Anyway, it wouldn't work. Ken is the stubbornest man I ever knew. He'd probably have whipped you if he'd been sober."

"Probably," Dan said. "Now let's get some sleep."

Amy lay staring upward into the absolute darkness of the prospector's cabin. She thought about what Dan had said, about how it was a miracle that she was still alive. Dan was right. It *was* a miracle.

"Are you married?" he asked out of the darkness.

"No. You?"

"No decent woman would marry a dead-broke prospector like me. Not if she was in her right mind."

"Maybe you won't always be broke."

"Maybe," he said. "I got a feeling about this claim I'm working here. I'm about sixty feet into the side of the mountain and damned if the quartz doesn't look promising."

48

"My father told me that the presence of quartz sometimes indicates gold."

"That's true and maybe this is just one of those times. I've been working like a slave for almost three months here and I just have a feeling in my bones that this claim might finally pay off."

"I hope it does," Amy said. "And I hope that someone comes and gets me before long so that I'm not a drain on your food and water supply."

"Aw," he scoffed, "don't you worry a thing about that. If worse comes to worst, we can always eat my burro."

"*Eat* him?"

"Sure! Burros don't cost a lot. They can be a terrible pain sometimes and this one is plenty troublesome. I call him Biscuit because that's his favorite food. He'd rather eat a biscuit than a bowl of sugar."

"I see," Amy said. "Well, I'm sure that we won't have to eat him."

"Don't tell him that," Dan said in a serious voice. "He behaves better if I keep a little fear working in his ornery heart."

Despite the way she felt, Amy had to smile into the darkness at that comment. She knew from the stories how prospectors, especially loners like Dan, often began to think of their burros as people, carrying on conversations with them and even getting into some deep and philosophical discussions.

"'Night, Dan. And thanks for saving my life."

"You're plenty welcome," he said with a yawn. "When I came upon that coach and what was left of those poor horses, I couldn't believe that anyone or anything survived. But then I saw your leg sticking out from under some busted up wood and when I pushed it aside, there

49

you were, a livin' and breathin' angel."

"I've never been an angel."

"Well," Dan said, "there must have been a couple of angels sitting on your shoulder when that coach went around the corner and flew off the mountainside. There's no other way to account for you still being alive."

"And you really got a good look at the man who tried to finish me off?"

"I sure did. He was a mean-lookin' cuss. Was riding a bay horse with four white stockings. He looked to be a big fellow and was dressed mostly in black. If I see him again, I'll not hesitate to go for my gun."

"Me neither," Amy said. "But I'm not sure that I can remember what he looked like."

"I'd be surprised if you could," Dan said. "You got a couple of knots on your pretty head."

Amy closed her eyes. She felt safe here with Dan. Somewhere out in this high-desert country with its rugged piñon and juniper studded peaks was a killer who would come to finish her off so that she could never identify him in a court of law. But Dan knew that and he was prepared to fight for her.

And she liked him, even if he had whipped her brother.

★

Chapter 7

Amy awoke to see sunlight streaming through the cabin's open door. For several minutes, she lay still, listening, and then she steeled herself for the pain that she knew movement would bring, and slowly eased into a sitting position.

The pain was not as bad as Amy had expected. That probably had a lot to do with the very professional manner in which Dan had wrapped her side wound and immobilized her badly bruised and cracked ribs. Amy eased her legs off the bed and set her next goal, which would be to walk across the room and out the door. She wanted to feel the warmth of the sun and to find Dan.

Walking was painful but Amy gritted her teeth and walked anyway, or rather, shuffled to the open door.

The sun did feel wonderful. At these high elevations, the temperature never became too hot in the summertime, and Amy could smell the delicious scent of the surrounding pine trees. There was little to see except the cabin and, nearby, Biscuit, the troublesome burro that Dan had jokingly suggested they might eat if they ran out of food.

Amy slowly moved over to the burro who was neither tethered nor corralled. The little, flop-eared critter was quite old, from the looks of him. Biscuit's face was covered with gray hair and he had the largest and saddest eyes that Amy had ever seen in an animal.

"How old *are* you?" she asked, scratching Biscuit behind his drooping ears.

The burro sighed with enjoyment. He closed his eyes and his head dropped a few inches. As Amy scratched, she began to think that the cute little old fellow had already dozed off.

"Enough of this," Amy said, looking around for the mine shaft where she would find Dan working.

She did not have to search long or hard. The mine shaft was easy enough to spot because of a big yellowish and red pile of tailings. The tailings sparkled quartz and, as Amy moved toward the shaft, she was reminded of Dan's optimism regarding the hoped for vein of gold.

She could hear Dan inside, grunting and pounding on the face of the rock. Never one to like climbing into pits or shafts, Amy elected to wait outside. She leaned up against a pine tree putting her weight mostly on her left side, and closed her eyes. She knew she should have felt miserable, given all the death and heartache that she had seen and suffered, but right now, mostly she just felt gratitude. Dan had been right when he'd said it was a miracle that she was still alive.

Several minutes later, Dan appeared pushing a wheelbarrow filled with loose rock. When he saw Amy, he dropped the wheelbarrow and it almost capsized.

"What are you doing out of bed!"

"I came to visit," Amy said, surprised by his sharp

tone of voice. "I'm not going to lie in bed until someone comes to find me. I'm not in *that* bad of shape."

Suddenly, he smiled. "I know *exactly* what kind of shape you are in, Miss Ross. And you're right, you are in remarkably good shape."

His eyes bored into her and although Amy tried to hold his glance, she had to look away because she knew that she was blushing.

"What do you think of my old friend, Biscuit?" he asked.

"How old is he?"

"I don't know. Perhaps twenty years. Maybe even older. It's my sourdough biscuits that keep him alive, you know."

"Of course," Amy said. "What else?"

"You shouldn't be standing on your feet so long," he said. "And if you don't want to go back to bed, then you should at least sit."

"Where?"

"Here," he replied, dumping the wheelbarrow and then quickly piling the rock up to a small pedestal.

Amy eyed it skeptically. "It doesn't look very stable."

"Oh, but it is!" To demonstrate, Dan sat down on the pile of rocks and even crossed his legs. "See?"

"It looks uncomfortable, too."

Dan chuckled and before Amy could stop him, he removed his shirt, which he then folded and placed on the top of the pile. "Now," he said rather proudly, "you even have a seat cushion."

"Thank you!"

Amy sat on the pile of rocks while Dan excused himself with an airy, "Got to keep working, my dear."

And he really did work. Every fifteen or twenty

minutes, while Amy sat and waited, Dan would emerge from the tunnel with another load of rock to dump on his pile of tailings. This went on all morning and, finally, Dan stopped and said, "I think we are probably both getting hungry."

"As a matter of fact, I'm starving!"

"You ought to be."

Amy frowned. "What do you mean?"

"I mean," Dan said, "that you were unconscious for two days."

Amy blinked. "Two whole days!"

"And a night."

This revelation would have staggered Amy had she not been sitting down. "I had no idea."

"Like I said," Dan told her, "you took some very nasty knocks on the head. I was almost certain that you had a severe concussion. I'm glad that proved not to be the case."

"You seem to know something about medicine."

"I went to the Boston College of Medicine. They even allowed me to graduate."

"You're a college-educated doctor?"

"That's right."

"But . . ."

His smile faded. "Please don't ask. It's a long and not a happy story. Suffice to say, I left the practice of medicine and came to Nevada for the solitude."

"And the gold."

"Yes," he admitted, "I hope to strike it rich. And I've got the fever as bad as any of 'em."

"What would you do if you did strike it rich?"

"I'd build a frontier hospital out here someplace in the wild mining camps of Nevada."

"And get right back into medicine."

"Exactly," he said rather cheerfully. "I know that none of it makes a bit of sense. But no matter. I *am* a doctor and I needed time away from people and patients."

"And then I came into your life and now you've both."

"For a while," he said. "Until we either leave or a search party finds us, though I don't expect that to happen."

"And why not?"

"When I found you, I was returning from Austin with a year's worth of supplies."

Amy waited, not sure what she was expected to say. Finally, she said, "And?"

"The point is that we traveled some distance from the stagecoach wreck and I don't think we'll be found right away."

"But surely your tracks . . ."

"In the summer, we often get some pretty violent thundershowers up in these mountains."

Now she finally understood what he was driving at. "So," she said slowly. "You don't want to leave and you don't think we'll soon be found."

"I don't think that you're in any shape to travel for at least a couple of weeks," he said. "A ride over to Austin in the burro cart would be extremely painful and your cracked rib might suffer further damage."

Amy sighed. "And it appears that Biscuit is far too small, weak, and old for me to ride."

"Exactly."

Amy took a deep breath. "It kind of sounds as if I'm trapped here with you for a while."

"Is that so terrible?" he asked. "I am an honorable man. I give you my word that I will behave like a gentleman."

55

Amy smiled. "I believe you, Dr. Smith, or whatever your name is. It's just that I came out here to find out what happened to my father and brother."

"They're dead," he told her.

"But maybe not Ken," she added quickly.

Dan did not argue the point but it was clear from his expression that he thought Ken dead. "I understand your reason for coming and I marvel at your resilience and courage. You killed two highwaymen and survived a wreck that I'd have sworn no one could have lived through. However, you need rest and recuperation and . . . well, I need some female companionship and a few weeks to find out rather I've really hit a bonanza or if it's just another *borrasca.*"

"*Borrasca* meaning . . ."

"A bust," Dan said. "It's a Mexican term. Bonanza means you strike it rich, *borrasca* means your claim is a worthless bust. The Mexicans hold a strong belief that, as many days as you work in *borrasca*, so many days shall you be in bonanza."

"They really believe that?"

"They certainly do," Dan insisted. "At least they used to until they went to work in the old Central Mine up in Virginia City for Superintendent Frank."

"What do you mean?"

"The Central Mine was once very productive but it went *borrasca*. After months and months of no ore, Frank ran out of money to pay his crews. He was ready to shut the mine down until the Mexicans came and offered to work it for free—but only if they could work for themselves as many days in bonanza as they did in *borrasca*."

Amy smiled. "And so what did Mr. Frank have to

56

lose? If he refused the offer, he had nothing to gain, but even if the Mexicans struck it rich and found a bonanza, he would at least have something."

"Exactly," Dan said. "Or so he thought. He agreed to the bargain and the Mexicans went to work. Frank thought they would quit after a few days, or possibly a week. But they had such faith in their belief that they would hit a bonanza and become rich that they continued to work—for months."

Dan chuckled. "As time went on, and the Mexicans showed no sign of quitting—even though they worked for free—Frank became more and more concerned."

"But why?"

"He realized that, should the Mexicans really strike a big bonanza, they would have enough time to strip it clean for themselves, and he would get nothing."

"I see! Did he fire them?"

"How could he?" Dan asked. "He had made a deal with the Mexicans that they could work in *borrasca* as long as they wished."

Amy chuckled. "So what finally happened?"

"Frank became so upset and agitated over the prospect of losing a fortune to the Mexicans that he went to see a one-eyed old Castilian who was supposed to be the greatest mining expert on the Comstock Lode."

"To ask him if there was going to be a big strike?"

"Yes." Dan grinned. "And do you know what the Castilian said?"

"No," Amy said, enjoying the story, "but I have a strong feeling that you are about to tell me."

"The Castilian went down in the mine and gave it a thorough examination. He crawled through all the drifts, the crosscuts and he even took ore samples. His verdict was, a simple, *'nada bonanza'* meaning, the Central

57

Mine was bust and that it would never again produce gold or silver."

"Did this make Mr. Frank happy, or sad?"

"Happy. Very happy." Dan shook his head. "You see, it's human nature that most of us would rather gain nothing in the first place than gain big and then lose everything."

Amy laughed because there was more than a measure of truth to Dan's words.

"Let's go find something to eat," Dan said, taking her arm and supporting her as they started back toward the cabin.

They were halfway there when Biscuit suddenly raised his head up and began to bray fitfully, throwing his sad brown eyes toward the eastern hills surrounding the cabin.

Amy frowned. "What . . ."

"He's found us!" Dan shouted as a rifle shot boomed from up in the hills. Before Amy could even react, Dan scooped her off the ground and ran for the cabin. He was almost there when the second shot sent him and Amy both tumbling.

"Dan!" she cried.

"Get inside!"

"Not without you," she vowed, forgetting her own wounds as she grabbed the doctor and pulled him into the cabin with bullets spraying the dirt all around them.

They had barely gotten inside when Biscuit's braying suddenly ended in mid-note. "He shot Biscuit!" Dan swore. "The bastard killed my burro!"

"Where are you hit?"

Dan grabbed his leg. "It's just a flesh wound. I'm going after that sonofabitch and make him pay for this!"

Jumping to his feet, Dan hobbled over to snatch up

his rifle. He checked to make sure that it was loaded and when he looked up, Amy saw that his cheeks were wet with tears for the loss of his pet burro.

"Dan, please, don't do anything foolish."

"Not on your life. This man isn't going away until he is dead, or he's killed us both. Amy, you arm yourself just in case . . . in case things don't work out right."

Amy nodded. She knew that the doctor was correct. They could run, and they could not hide. The ambusher and highwayman had too much at stake to just ride away from this trouble. He would fight them to the death.

Amy felt her stomach knot with fear and worry. She rushed over to Dan and hugged his neck. "*Please* be careful!"

"I will. And don't worry, I do know how to use a rifle."

"I never doubted that for a minute," Amy said as the doctor went to the door, then suddenly bolted into the nearest pines and disappeared up a shallow draw where he would at least initially be protected from the ambusher who meant to kill them both.

Chapter 8

Dan moved as quickly as he could up the arroyo knowing that he was probably going up against a superior marksman. His leg was bleeding and when he looked down and saw how much blood he was losing, he was shocked. In a very short while, he would begin to weaken from blood loss and that meant that he needed to kill this ambusher in a hurry. To do that, he would have to take chances because time was not his ally.

About a hundred yards up the arroyo, he flattened and then crawled up to where he could have a better look at his surroundings, thinking, Where is he?

Dan waited for several minutes, hoping that the ambusher would show himself, but when he did not, Dan started upward again, trying to keep close to the lip of the arroyo. He went about another thirty-five yards when some inner sense told him to freeze.

He heard the sound of a rock tumbling through brush. It sounded very close. Dan wiped cold sweat from his eyes and took a deep, steadying breath. The rifle in his fists felt as slick as if it had been greased. Dan swallowed and was sure the sound of it could be heard by his enemy.

Suddenly, he saw movement in the sagebrush about sixty yards up the mountainside. It quickly became apparent that the ambusher was inching down the same arroyo, his full concentration focused on the cabin below. Dan raised his rifle and took aim. He could not see the ambusher clearly because he was shielded by brush, but there was enough of a target to warrant taking a shot.

"Freeze!" Dan ordered.

The ambusher *did* freeze, for about a heartbeat. Then, the man swung around with his own rifle and fired without even taking aim. Dan saw a muzzle blast, and felt as if a finger of death snaked out and touched his cheek. A piece of sage exploded in front of his eyes as a bullet whistled past his face. Dan squeezed his own trigger and saw the ambusher jerk spasmodically as a slug struck the ambusher high in the left shoulder.

The man howled and his rifle spilled from his hands, but he drew his six-gun and began to fire. Dan rolled sideways in panic and crashed down the side of the arroyo. He momentarily lost his own rifle as another bullet plucked at his sleeve. Dan clutched at the rifle, and when he had it solidly in his fists, he levered in another shell and squeezed off another shot. This time, his slug punched the ambusher low in the chest and Dan didn't need a medical school education to realize that the fight was over. The man grunted and collapsed with his pistol coughing slugs into the dirt.

Dan jumped up and scrambled over to the dying man. He rolled the ambusher onto his back and stared into his rapidly glazing eyes.

"Who are you?"

"You . . . you sonofabitch!" the ambusher choked. "You went and killed me!"

"You gave me no choice! Are you one of the men who robbed that stagecoach and killed everyone except Miss Ross?"

The man's lips pulled away from his teeth. They were covered with a crimson froth and his gums were white as his heart pumped away his life's blood.

"I . . ."

Dan leaned closer and the ambusher tried to spit on him, then died with a terrible shudder.

"You deserved what you got," Dan said, pushing to his feet and swaying at the bottom of the arroyo. "And I have no use for the likes of you. You'll get no more of a burial from me than you gave to the stagecoach guard and driver."

Dan pivoted around. He expelled a deep sigh of relief knowing that he was very fortunate simply to be alive.

"Dan!"

He looked up to see Amy scrambling up the arroyo. Her eyes darted to the dead man and then she threw her arms around Dan, hugging him fiercely.

"Thank God that you're alive!"

"Let's get down to the cabin," Dan said, using her for support. "We're both pretty banged up but lucky to have survived."

"Yes," she whispered, helping him along. "When I heard the shots just now, I thought . . ."

He forced a grin that did not come easy. "You didn't have much faith in me, did you Amy?"

"It's not that. It's just that you're a *doctor* while the man that you were up against was a killer. I just felt that he had every advantage."

63

"It appears that neither one of us is very easy to kill," Dan told her with a grimace.

Once they were inside the cabin, Amy set him down on the edge of the bed and said, "Now it's my turn to examine you, Dr. Smith. I can either cut your pants leg up to your crotch, or you can remove your pants and we'll have a look. Which is it to be?"

"I only own two pair and I can sew up a lousy bullet hole," he grated, pushing to his feet. "I'll take them off."

And he did. Unfortunately, Dan was still wearing his long underwear under his pants and those had to be removed as well. The whole process was painful and time consuming. Amy fretted because Dan was losing blood and she suspected that his wound was worse than he was willing to admit.

"There," she said, cutting the long underwear open and pulling the blood-soaked material aside.

"See," he said, "just a crease."

"A very *deep* crease!"

"There's some sulfa powder in my medical kit," he told her. "But first boil some water and cleanse the wound, then dry it and put on the powder and I'll show you how to wrap it tight enough to stop the flow of blood but not so tight as to cut off the circulation to my feet."

"Which would be bad?"

"Very bad," he assured her.

Amy did everything he wanted and when she had finished binding the wound, he favored her with a compliment. "A lot of young ladies might have swooned or simply refused. You didn't. I respect that."

"My father taught me a little about life," Amy replied.

"I've never been sheltered from the realities of the world."

"I see."

"You need to lie down and . . ."

"I need a tall glass of whiskey," he told her. "And it wouldn't hurt you to have the same. It's not every day that one survives an ambush."

"I agree. Where do you hide the bottle?"

He told her where to find his stock of whiskey and a couple of clean glasses. Amy poured them four fingers each in a water glass and sat down beside him on the bed.

"To life," she said.

"And to health," he added.

They drank. The whiskey was surprisingly smooth compared to the whiskey that her father and brother had usually consumed. "Where did you get this?"

"It comes from Tennessee," he replied.

"Did *you* come from Tennessee?"

"As a matter of fact, I did," he said. "My father was a southern plantation owner in Georgia. When he saw first seeds of a civil war, he sold his plantation and we moved to a place near the Blue Ridge Mountains. We raised Thoroughbred horses and lived a pretty idyllic life."

"But you left it. Why?"

"After the war was over and I was a man, I went north to medical school. My intention was to return to Tennessee and attend some of the soldiers who had lost their health and their limbs during the fighting."

"But . . ."

"I did go back for a few years," he said. "And I fell in love and even married. My wife . . ."

Amy heard a small choking sound deep in his throat and she placed her hand on his shoulder. "Please, Dan,

65

you don't need to talk about it if the memories are too painful. I didn't mean to pry."

"My wife died in childbirth and I couldn't save her or my son. I made a bad decision and it proved fatal for both of them."

"You did your best."

"And it wasn't nearly good enough," he said bitterly.

"But . . ."

"After they were gone," he said, his voice dropping to a whisper, "I became disillusioned and haunted by what had happened. I ran to the West and, for a time, even tried to lose myself in this harsh wilderness. When I had to go among people, I lost myself in . . . in other ways."

"I see."

"No," he said softly, "you *don't* see, and for that I am very grateful. I became something of which I was not very proud."

"You were suffering and in pain," she said. "You were overwhelmed by guilt."

"Yes." He had been staring at his hands but now he raised his head and looked into her eyes. "A year ago, I was in another situation where I was able to use my medical training and skills to save a human being, a mother in childbirth."

"Out here?"

"That's right. She was a young Paiute Indian woman with her first child. It was twisted and she would surely have died had I not been available. I was able to turn the baby and help her have a normal delivery. The Paiutes don't forget something like that. I'm surprised that they have not come here since I've returned with you seeking my help and medicine."

Amy sighed. Now, she understood this man. He had

run from his home in Tennessee seeking oblivion and had found, instead, a purpose for which to live again.

"I admire you very much," she confessed, wrapping her arms around his neck and kissing him on the lips.

His eyes were shining with tears and he crushed her to his breast, then they lay back on the bed. "Amy," he whispered, "I have not even wanted to touch another woman since my wife and son died four years ago. But I was drawn to you the moment I laid eyes upon you and you have filled my thoughts ever since. I . . . I am quite serious when I say that it's a revelation to me that I would even want another woman. But I do."

"And I want you," she said without reservation as she ran her hands over his hard, slender body. "I owe you my life."

"I don't want gratitude," he said, gazing into her eyes. "I want your love."

"Take it," she breathed, feeling her heart begin to pound with excitement.

Amy forgot about her cracked ribs just as he forgot about his leg wound. She couldn't get out of her dress fast enough and it took them less than a minute to peel off every last stitch of their clothing. He was hard and hungry and when she opened her legs wide, he impaled her with his stiff rod.

"Oh," Amy moaned, feeling him go deep inside of her and begin to thrust with hard strokes. "Yes!"

Amy hugged his neck and her fingernails worked up and down his backbone as he worked over her, his voice already growing ragged with passion. For her own part, Amy could feel fire in her loins and she realized that she was also gasping as a wave of pleasure lifted her higher and higher.

"Oh, Doctor," she breathed, "you feel so good!"

He laughed and thrust even harder until Amy began to buck and thrust back at him and her head rolled from side to side. Moments later, they were both crying out with pleasure as their bodies exploded with sweet, shuddering relief. Amy hugged him tightly as he filled her with torrents of his hot seed. And when he sobbed, she knew that she had given him a healing that went far beyond the mere physical.

"I don't want you to leave," he panted, hugging her tightly.

"I have to," she told him. "When they come and find us, I have to go on to Eureka and find out what happened to my father and my brother."

"Then I'm coming with you."

Amy smiled and rocked him in her warm, wet cradle hoping that her rescuers would not find her too soon.

★

Chapter 9

When Jessie and Ki reached Austin, Nevada, the first thing they did was to ride their horses over to the stageline office and inquire about Amy Ross.

The man in charge was sitting behind his desk and there was a wooden plaque that read O.A. POLLARD, OPERATIONS MANAGER. Pollard was a small, intense-looking man who chewed big cigars and was constantly spitting tobacco into a brass cuspidor. When Jessie and Ki entered his cramped and untidy office, Pollard was busy writing a report of some kind and he didn't even bother to glance up from his pad and pencil.

"Mr. Pollard?"

"I'm busy," the man growled. "You can buy a ticket when you board the stage."

"We don't want to buy tickets," Jessie said, pushing back her dusty Stetson and shaking out her hair. "We're looking for Miss Amy Ross. She was a passenger on a stage that must have arrived here yesterday or possibly the day before and . . ."

Something in Pollard's stricken expression caused Jessie's words to die on her lips.

"That was Miss Ross? George Ross's daughter?"

"That's right," Jessie said. "Is something wrong?"

Pollard's pencil dropped from his fingers and he pushed back in his office chair. "Would you and your friend care to take a couple of seats?"

"No!" Jessie said, really getting alarmed. "Is there something wrong?"

Pollard spat tobacco juice into his cuspidor and wiped his lips with the back of his sleeve. His teeth were badly stained and there were dark circles under his eyes. He looked unwell to Jessie.

"The stage that Miss Ross was on was attacked by robbers about fifteen miles west of here. When that run didn't come in, we sent out a search party, thinking that maybe an axle had broken or something like that. But the truth of the matter is that the coach was attacked and wrecked."

Jessie felt her insides go cold. "Was Amy . . ."

"She's missing," Pollard said quickly. "We found the wreck down at the bottom of a ravine. It had tumbled off a mountainside. We found the bodies of the driver and the guard about a mile away and there was a passenger named Delbert Denton. We almost didn't find his body in the rubble."

Jessie sat down heavily. "Did you search the wreckage well enough so that there is no possibility that Amy was killed?"

"Yes, ma'am! There were four dead horses and that Denton fella that I told you about and nothing else."

"What could have happened to her?" Ki asked.

Pollard shook his head. "I've been asking myself that same damned question over and over. The only thing

70

that I can figure is that whoever attacked that coach must have forced the woman to go with them. I don't have to tell you the most likely reasons why she was the only one whose life was spared."

Ki looked to Jessie, who said, "What about tracks?"

"There was a hell of a thunder-buster and it washed everything out clean."

"Was there even a search party?" Jessie asked, unable to hide her anger.

"Of course there was! I closed the office and rounded up every able and willing man in Austin. We paid them cash to join in the hunt and we searched all day yesterday. But, ma'am, we didn't find a clue. It was like the country just swallowed them up whole."

"Where is the wreckage site?" Jessie asked.

"You wouldn't have seen it from the road because it was way down in a canyon, but you passed it on the way in," Pollard said. "And as for where them murderers went . . . oh, I almost forgot to mention something important."

"And that is?"

"Two highwaymen were shot dead," Pollard said with obvious satisfaction. "We found their bodies on the road near where the guard and the driver had been gunned down."

"Could you even tell how many robbers were in the gang?" Ki asked.

"Nope. Like I said, there was a hell of a cloudburst and we got about three inches of rain in an hour. It just washed out all signs. In fact, it even washed out the wheel-cuts where the coach went off the road and over the mountainside. We almost missed it entirely."

"Is there any chance that she might have walked away from the wreck and gone on to Eureka?"

Pollard frowned. "I doubt it. Why do you ask?"

"Because," Jessie explained, "Amy was determined to get to Eureka in order to find out what happened to her father and her brother. To my way of thinking, that's where she would have gone if she'd have survived."

"Without even coming into Austin and telling us about the attack and the wreck?" Pollard shook his head. "Doesn't seem very likely to me."

Ki leaned a little toward Jessie. "I could search for Amy, if you think you need to go on to Eureka."

"If she's alive and free, that's where she'd go," Jessie said with complete conviction. "She might even have been captured and then somehow managed to escape."

"You could go to Eureka and I could try to find Amy. One way or the other, we could meet in Eureka and see if we can get to the bottom of her father's death and her brother's disappearance."

Jessie nodded her head. She knew that alone Ki could travel faster and cover much more ground. And yet, the temptation to go hunt for Amy was almost irresistible.

"You ain't going to find her," Pollard vowed. "We went over that rough country with a fine comb and there's not a sign of that young woman, believe you me."

But Jessie wasn't listening. She and Ki were moving out the door, making plans.

"We need to rest our horses and ourselves tonight," Jessie told the samurai. "If we don't give our mounts a good graining and rest tonight, they may either play out or go lame in the next few days and that would be a disaster."

"Agreed."

Jessie gazed up and down the busy streets of Austin. The town was slightly past its prime and the boom was over, but Austin still retained the vestiges of wealth. There were two big hotels and a goodly number of excellent places to eat. Most of the mining town was built on the slopes of hills and the streets were steep and narrow.

"The last time we held over in this town we stayed at the Bonanza House," Jessie said. "Let's put our horses up at the livery and then see if we can get rooms at the Bonanza House again."

"That shouldn't be a problem," Ki said. "It looks to me as if about a third of the businesses in town have been boarded up since we were here last."

Jessie had the same impression. Austin was the county seat and so it was unlikely that the town would wither away and die, even if the last of the mining companies folded. And there were some big cattle operations in the rough, sage-covered lands surrounding Austin that employed a fair number of buckaroos.

Since there was only one livery in town that appeared to be in full operation, Jessie and Ki wasted little time in making arrangements for their weary mounts.

"We'll be leaving early in the morning," Jessie explained, "and I want these animals in good shape."

The liveryman cocked his eyebrow and squinted over a corn-cob pipe. He appeared to be in his early sixties, crusty and feisty as a fighting bantam rooster.

"Every horse that comes to my livery leaves in better condition than it arrived," he said. "And these horses are plumb worn out. They ought to be kept here for at least three days."

"I'm afraid," Jessie said, "that is just not possible. Just grain them heavily and have them curried to a shine. I also want you to check their shoes and make sure that none are loose."

"I'll do that, but it'll cost you two bits extra."

"Fine," Jessie said, handing the man a silver dollar. "I expect that will take care of everything."

The proprietor nodded. "Sure will. Where are you heading?"

"I'm going to Eureka," Jessie said. "My friend has other business to attend to."

"I see," the man said, clearly not seeing at all. "Well, sir, if you enjoy our town, might be that you'll come back through and spend a little more time."

"Might be," Ki said, taking Jessie's arm as they turned and walked away.

"We left him something to speculate and gossip about," Jessie said as they moved down the street. "That old fella was just dying to know what we are up to."

"And I'll bet he finds out from Pollard before tomorrow morning," Ki said. "It's hard to keep a secret in these small towns. Everyone knows everyone's business."

Jessie and Ki checked into the hotel and they each ordered hot baths. Jessie soaked for nearly an hour and then she went downstairs to meet the samurai.

Ki was not in the lobby. Jessie went over to the desk clerk and said, "You know Ki. Has he been down yet? We're supposed to meet here for dinner."

"He stepped out for a moment and told me to tell you that he'd be right back."

Jessie's eyebrows raised. "Did he give you any reason for leaving?"

"There was a man that wanted to speak privately with him. They went outside."

Jessie looked toward the door. She could probably step out and find Ki, but she decided that she would leave him to his own devices and go into the dining room. Ki would be along shortly.

The dining room was small and intimate with only about a dozen tables. Jessie was escorted into a nice corner and given a menu that was long on beefsteak, lamb and trout, and short on most everything else.

"My, my," a voice said. "As I live and breathe, it's Miss Jessica Starbuck of Texas!"

She looked up to see an old friend of Amy's father, Judge Roy Lantis, whom she had met on a few occasions. The judge was retired and well into his seventies. It was a mystery to Jessica why he had chosen to live in such a small outpost as Eureka when he could have enjoyed the benefits of Reno or Carson City, where he would have had a good deal more intellectual and cultural stimulation.

"May I join you?" the judge asked.

"By all means. I'm waiting for Ki and I know that he will enjoy seeing you as well."

"Ki is such a remarkable individual," the judge said, taking a seat across from her. "I have never seen anyone that could handle himself any better in a dangerous situation."

"Ki was trained by Hirata, who was a great samurai who had lost his master."

"His master?"

"That's right," Jessie said. "In Japan, when a samurai's master dies, it is almost expected that he will commit *seppuku*, which is the ancient Japanese ritual of disembowelment."

"They open up their own bellies?" the judge asked, looking a little appalled.

"With two clean cuts, both long and deep," Jessie said. "They use the *katana*, which is their long, ritual sword."

Jessie leaned back in her chair. "Anyway, Ki's mentor saved his life when he was a starving outcast in Japan. He raised him, taught him *kakuto bugei,* which is the true samurai's way, and then took his life as his own code of honor demanded."

"Would Ki commit *seppuku* if you were killed or died of some natural cause?"

"I have made him swear on his honor that he would not," Jessie said. "I want him to live long and well."

The judge nodded and when a waiter arrived, they ordered drinks and the judge said, "Does Ki still carry those funny little star blades that he uses instead of a gun?"

Jessie had to smile at that description. "Yes," she said. "They are called *shuriken* and they are far more deadly in his hands than a gun is in the hands of most men."

"Oh," Lantis said, "I believe that. I was in Carson City that time when he had to use one of them things in order to save the life of an innocent bystander who was about to be gunned down in a bank robbery. It was a sight that I'll never forget."

Jessie glanced over her shoulder. "Ki should be along any minute now. We are on our way to Eureka."

"Yeah," the judge said. "I had guessed as much. I'm sure that you want to find out everything that you can about the death of George and his son."

Jessie started with surprise. "Ken is dead?"

"Yeah," the judge said. "They found his body yesterday. He'd been dumped down a mine shaft, just like everyone figured."

Jessie shook her head. "What a tragedy! And now Amy herself is missing."

"I've been upset all day," the judge said, looking

76

very grim. "I just can't hardly believe that family's misfortunes."

"Do you think that the two men died because of a supposed gold mine?"

"No 'supposed' about it, Miss Starbuck," the judge said. "George and Ken both came by my house about a month ago and asked me to help them with some legal papers, which I do to supplement my meager retirement pay."

"You say legal papers?"

"That's right. They both wanted their wills drawn up and, of course, they both named Amy as their beneficiary. They told me they had struck it rich but, of course, not wanting to divulge anything more of the nature of their holdings, they did not tell me the location of the mine."

"I see." Jessie took a sip of the wine that had just arrived and frowned. "I wonder if anyone else knew about Amy being the beneficiary of that mine in the event that George and Ken were killed."

"I don't think so," the judge said. "You see, that would put Amy's life in some jeopardy. There are ruthless men who would think nothing of killing her as well and then claiming the mine for themselves."

"Which they could do if Amy were dead?"

"Certainly." The judge steepled his fingers. "You see, because George and Ken were unwilling to file a mining claim which would have made their mine's location a matter of public record, the mine does not legally belong to them. At least, not in the eyes of the State of Nevada. Now, if Amy is alive, and since the wills that I drew for both men are valid, she would inherit the mine and then have to file a formal claim."

"But," Jessie said, "if she is dead, then . . ."

77

"Then the mine belongs to anyone who can find and file on it first."

"I understand. What that means is that Amy could be in considerable danger."

"I would say so," the judge replied. "I wonder if the young woman is even aware of the precarious position she is in and if it had anything to do with her disappearance from the stagecoach."

"I don't know," Jessie said, "I sure hope not. I'm leaving for Eureka tomorrow morning while Ki is remaining to search for Amy. There are a lot of questions yet to be answered."

"I'm devastated by what has happened to the Ross family," the judge said, drinking his whiskey. "As you well know, I thought the world of George. Ken was, well, difficult and not a bit like his father, but certainly did not deserve to die."

"I don't suppose that there are any suspects."

The judge shook his head. "From what little I heard, they just found the body and there wasn't a clue. Of course, when a man falls or is thrown down one of those deep shafts, his body is probably torn to pieces bouncing off the shoring on the way down. And then, of course, there is the impact. I'm sure that there was not a lot left of either man by the time that they were found."

Jessie poured herself some of the judge's whiskey. "Tell me one thing," she said, taking a gulp and feeling the fiery liquor course down her throat, "did George or Ken give you any idea about even the general location of their find?"

"They were very secretive about that, even to me. But I recall they did say that it was near water."

"A spring? There are hundreds of them."

"No. A stream and George said that they had plenty of pines for timber and had built a cabin and were using the pine to shore up their mine."

"That isn't much help," Jessie said. "Did you get any indication how far it was from Eureka?"

"Two days ride," the judge said. "Yes. Once, Ken said that it took them two days to get to Eureka and one . . . yes! Two days to Austin."

"Now *that*," Jessie said, "is good information to know. Since Eureka is a very hard day's ride, I'd say about sixty miles east of us . . ."

"Maybe only fifty," the judge interrupted.

"Did George and Ken travel horseback, or afoot?"

"They had burros, same as most."

"Then that means they would make about twenty-five miles a day." Jessie took a deep breath. "I think what this all means is that we can draw a triangle with the base being the distance between Austin and Eureka. The top of the triangle would be northwest two days and so the Ross Mine would either be there, or else at the bottom of a triangle to the southeast. In both cases, two days distance to either Austin or Eureka."

"Sure makes sense," the judge said as he extracted a pen and piece of paper out of his pocket and drew a diamond-shaped figure. "But you know how rough and wild that country is. You'll find a few Indians and a lot of scorpions and tarantulas. You'll also find mustangs and jackrabbits. Not much else."

"Any streams or rivers come to mind?" Jessie asked, touching the top and the bottom points of the diamond.

"I don't know that country well enough to make a guess on that, but I'm sure that there are."

"Well," Jessie said, "I can find out about that after I get to Eureka. The first thing I'll want to do is to try and figure out who killed George and Ken."

"I would think," Lantis said, "that, if you find the mine, you'll also find the killers."

"Not necessarily," Jessie said. "I'm hoping that the murderers never learned the mine's location."

The judge frowned. "Well, I guess . . ."

Whatever the judge was about to guess was forgotten as a loud rifle-shot boomed outside the hotel. Jessie heard shouts, but she was already on her feet and sprinting across the lobby and out the front door.

"Ki!" she screamed, falling to her knees beside the samurai.

"Somebody ambushed him from across the street," a man said. "I didn't see nothing but a puff of gunsmoke, but I can tell you he used a big-bore rifle to do his dirty work."

"Find a doctor!" Jessie cried, tearing open the samurai's tunic and feeling for a pulse.

The pulse, when she finally located it, was feeble but steady. Ki had taken a slug in the back with such impact that the ball had passed completely through his body and exited through his rib cage. He was bleeding profusely and Jessie shouted for someone to get her bandages.

"Hurry!" she cried, trying to stanch the flow of blood with her bare hands.

Someone raced into the hotel and brought out a handful of clean, white linen napkins. Jessie stuffed them into Ki's wound and they managed to get the blood to stop flowing so heavily.

"Jessica?"

She recognized the judge's voice and looked up to hear him say, "There's no doctor in Austin."

"What!"

80

"The only one we have comes through once every few weeks and lives in Eureka."

"Damn!" Jessie railed. "I can't believe this!"

"Let's get Ki moved over to my house," the judge said. "I've got big house with extra rooms. You'll be a lot more comfortable there than in a hotel."

Jessie agreed. Ki was pale, but his breathing was regular and his pulse was still steady. "I don't think it hit the lung or anything vital," she whispered. "If it had, he'd already . . ." Jessie had to struggle to say it. "He'd already be gone."

The judge took over. He knew everyone in town and he ordered someone to find a makeshift stretcher and help carry the badly wounded samurai over to his house, which was just one block up the hill.

When Ki was finally made comfortable and Jessie had done everything she dared to insure that he did not bleed to death, she pulled a chair up beside the samurai and laid her head down on the bed.

"I can't believe this is happening," she choked. "First George, then Ken, then poor Amy turns up missing and now Ki is ambushed."

"It's got to be a conspiracy," the judge said. "It has to be more than a single individual that is doing all this."

"I'll find them," Jessie said through clenched teeth. "I'll find out who is behind all this and I'll make sure they either hang or they never breathe another free breath of air."

Judge Lantis placed his hand on her shoulder. "Can I bring you some coffee or anything else to drink? Perhaps some food would also . . ."

"No," Jessie said quickly because the thought of food was repellent to her now. An hour ago, she had been quite hungry, but no longer. All she yearned for was revenge.

"I'll be just down the hall in my study until eleven o'clock," the judge told her. "After that, I'll be retiring unless you need me for something."

"He's going to make it," Jessie said, looking at the samurai though misty eyes. "Ki is incredibly strong and possesses an almost indomitable will to live."

"That," the judge said, "goes without saying. I'm not a doctor, but I would think that he would have died by now if he were not already on the mend."

"I agree," Jessie said, "although there is no way to be sure how much internal bleeding is taking place. We'll both know what to expect by tomorrow morning."

"Good night," the judge said. "Would a bottle of whiskey help?"

"No," Jessie told him in a quiet voice. "But a prayer might."

"Then I shall speak to Him and put in a good word for our samurai friend."

"Thank you," Jessie said as the door closed and she was left alone with the unconscious samurai.

★

Chapter 10

Jessie didn't sleep much during the next three days that Ki alternately drifted in and out of consciousness. But she did get one small break and that was when Dr. Alton from Eureka showed up at the judge's house.

"Thank heavens you've come!" Jessie exclaimed with relief.

"The stagecoach driver gave me your message," Alton replied. "I was scheduled to be here anyway next week, but things were slow in Eureka and I wanted to offer my services at . . ."

"This way," Jessie said, ushering the middle-aged and rumpled-looking physician in to see Ki. "I think he's on the mend, but he lost a lot of blood."

Alton took a quick look at Ki, then opened his medical kit and pulled out a stethoscope. He listened to Ki's heartbeat for several moments and said, "Remarkable."

"What is remarkable?"

"His heart is beating at about fifty beats a minute.

That's incredibly slow. Is he . . ."

"Ki is a highly conditioned athlete," Jessie explained. "He actually runs just for the exercise and to keep himself in perfect physical condition."

"Well, that he is," the doctor said. "I've tended to some of the tough Paiute Indians, but even their pulse rate runs in the mid-sixties."

"Would you please take a look at the wound," Jessie said trying to hide her exasperation. Small talk about pulse rates could wait until later.

"Of course," the doctor said, turning his full attention back to the samurai, who was sleeping. "But I must remark that you did a nice job of bandaging this man's wounds."

"Thanks."

Jessie watched as the doctor removed her bandages. She had to help him turn Ki and when the wounds were exposed, the doctor studied them very carefully.

"No sign of suppuration. The wounds appear to be healing very cleanly and without infection. Have you been using medicine?"

"The judge was able to provide me with some sulfa and tinctures."

"Very effective," the doctor said. "I can tell you right now that this man should make a full and complete recovery."

"Thank God!"

"However," Alton added, "it is going to take some time. Not only must the exterior tissues heal, but so must the interior tissues. In some cases, those can be the most delicate."

"Meaning?"

"Meaning this man cannot be moved for at least two weeks."

This news did not come to Jessie as a great surprise. She had been worried right from the beginning that a sixty-mile ride to Eureka over bumpy, rutted roads might prove too dangerous for Ki and reopen his wounds.

"Then we'll stay put until there is no question about Ki being able to be moved without risk."

Dr. Alton reached for fresh bandages. "That would be my advice. Why take chances?"

"Exactly."

Alton remained only about another half hour. He applied his own medicinal powder on the wounds and then he rebandaged them tightly saying, "I would continue to change the dressings at least twice a day for the next week."

"Will you be around?"

"I have to return to Eureka tomorrow," the doctor said. "I have a woman about ready to deliver her first baby. She is smallish and her husband is a big man. I fear that she might have complications and I want to be close at hand as the hour of the delivery approaches."

"I understand." Jessie went to her bag and pulled out a double eagle. "Will this repay you for coming over here to see Ki?"

"Amply," the doctor said with a quick grin. "And when I return next week, we can see how your friend is doing and perhaps even make arrangements for him to be moved to Eureka, if that is your wish and he is recovering as expected."

"Very good," Jessie said, feeling almost weak with relief.

The doctor started to leave but then he stopped at the door and turned. "By the way, I understand that you are a friend of the Ross family."

"I am."

"What a tragedy. First the father, then the daughter, then the son. All gone."

"Amy is still alive," Jessie said without thinking about it. "I . . . I can't tell you how I know that to be true, but it is."

"I certainly hope so. And I hope that a way can be found to bring their killers to a swift and lethal justice. This kind of thing simply cannot be allowed."

"I agree," Jessie said. "Did you examine both bodies?"

"I did," Alton said. "But there wasn't much to examine. Both men were disfigured almost beyond recognition."

"Beaten?"

"I couldn't tell," Alton admitted. "They were either beaten, or simply were torn apart by the fall and the impact when they hit the bottom of the mine shafts. Either way . . . well, it was very bad."

"Had they been robbed?"

"Robbed? You mean of their watches and things?"

"Yes."

"They had nothing of value on their persons."

"What about their personal belongings? They must have left behind something."

"Burros and packs. They were both very close-mouthed. We had all heard the rumors of a great strike they had made somewhere north of Eureka."

"Did you say north?"

"That's right. But . . ."

"How do you know that?"

"They came in from the north. Always."

Jessie thought that might just as well mean that the two Ross men had a mine to the south and only arrived at

Eureka after circling the town in order to mislead anyone who might be inclined to search for their gold mine.

"Thank you, Doctor."

"I'll be returning once more before I go back to Eureka," he said. "Just to make sure."

Jessie let the man out and then she met Judge Lantis in the hall and they both went into the study. Jessie told the judge what the doctor had said about George and Ken always arriving in Eureka on the north end of town.

"I agree with you," the judge said. "George Ross would do something like that. To my mind, it indicates that his mine is probably to the south."

That afternoon, Ki awakened and was fully aware of his surroundings for the very first time.

"Hi there," Jessie said. "You've had a long journey."

"But I am back," Ki said, looking around the room.

"Do you have any idea who ambushed you?"

"No. But I will recognize the man that drew me out so that I would make a better target. He said his name was Steve Hanson, and that he had some information about George Ross. I should never have stepped out where I was visible to an ambusher."

"And you can about bet that the man's name wasn't Steve Hanson," Jessie said.

"It doesn't matter," Ki told her. "I'll find him sooner or later."

Jessie told the samurai the news that Ken Ross was definitely dead. She ended by saying, "The doctor told me that he was nearly unrecognizable when they pulled him out of a mine shaft. Whoever killed Ken and his father is as cold-blooded as they come, and they're going to be looking for Amy."

"Then we need to find her first," Ki said.

"No," Jessie added in a soft voice, "I need to find her.

The doctor said that you would be risking your life if you traveled for another couple of weeks."

Protest reared up in Ki's dark eyes. "But I can't just stay here in bed!"

"I'm afraid that you'll have to," Jessie said. "Your wounds are healing nicely, but the doctor says that the inside tissue might well separate and that you could bleed to death internally if you were jarred or suffered any kind of fall."

Ki looked away quickly and Jessie knew how difficult it was for the samurai to accept his incapacitation, even for a few weeks. He turned his eyes to her and said, "So what are you going to do?"

"I'm going to hunt for Amy until I find her," Jessie said.

"But . . ."

"I promise you that I'll be careful," Jessie said, silencing his protest. "And I'll not be going all that far away."

"Amy's trail might run cold," Ki said. "Or it might lead hundreds of miles in any direction."

Jessie told the samurai how she had about determined that the Ross mine would be located two days ride south, southeast.

"But that doesn't mean that is where you will find Amy."

"If she was taken hostage in the hope of forcing her to tell them where her father's gold mine is located, that's where they'd go," Jessie said.

"And if she was dazed and merely wandered off to die in the wilderness?"

Jessie's expression turned wintery. "If that's the case, then there is nothing to do but to find the men who killed her and her family. And that we must do."

88

"Agreed," Ki said. He tried to push himself erect but even Ki's stoic control broke and his face went pale as he gritted his teeth in agony.

"I told you that the wound was serious," Jessie chided her friend. "The doctor said that very few men could have survived it and he was amazed at your slow pulse rate."

"How nice," Ki said, looking very dejected. "And now I am supposed to lie here while you risk your life out in the desert, probably against the same men who are at the root of all this trouble."

"I'll be all right," Jessie promised. "And I'll find a way to report back to you every few days."

"I need even more," Ki said. "I need you to promise me that, if you find these men, you will return to me and not try to capture or kill them without my help."

Jessie nodded her head in agreement. She touched the samurai's cheek and said, "You know that I wouldn't do anything foolish."

"What I know," Ki said, "is that you have the courage of a cornered badger."

"And you don't?"

Ki had to smile at that and Jessica left him that way. She went back to her hotel room, locked her door and quickly undressed and prepared for bed. Early in the morning she would begin the search for Amy. This would probably be the last night in quite some time that she would have the luxury of sleeping in a real bed. She realized that she'd better enjoy it because the trail that she would take might prove very long, hot and dangerous.

★

Chapter 11

The man named Modesto dismounted and handed his reins to one of the other five riders. His horse, a tall buckskin, sighed and lowered its head, flanks dripping with sweat. Modesto removed a pair of binoculars from his saddlebags and climbed about fifty feet to the crest of a ridge. Squatting on his haunches, the outlaw begin to study every inch of the vast range of mountains and desert in his field of vision.

Modesto lost track of time. He might have been looking through the binoculars for an hour, or just ten minutes. But either way, when he came to his feet, his face was grim and the corners of his mouth twisted downward. He marched back to his men and horses and jerked his reins free.

"We'll find her," he said. "I don't care if it takes another week, we're going to find her."

"Maybe," one of the gang members named Wilson offered, "Ross's daughter just crawled out of that stagecoach wreck and wandered off to die somewheres."

"Then we'd have found her by now."

"Unless she was eaten by coyotes."

"Then we'd have found her bones."

"Unless they were chewed up and scattered by the smaller animals," Wilson added.

Modesto glanced up at the man and when he spoke, his voice was flat and hard. "Even if she was eaten and her bones scattered, we'd have found *something*. Clothes, a shoe, a buckle or a piece of jewelry, some gawdamn thing!"

Wilson looked away, face angry and red.

"Someday," a heavyset man named Tyler chuckled, "you're going to learn to keep your damn mouth shut before Modesto bites it off."

"Shut up!" Wilson swore, sawing on his reins and riding off a ways to seethe by himself.

"You got any idea which direction they might have gone?" Tyler asked.

"We figured that the Ross mine is to the south but we already combed that damned part of the country. The girl must have been dazed or something and just started walking. I . . . I dunno where the hell she went. I just hope we can find her before she dies out here."

"Her chances aren't looking good," the man said. "It's been what, almost a week since that coach was wrecked."

"That's right," Modesto snapped. "But we know she was young and I hope strong."

"And maybe good-lookin'," another one of the men said, his eyes hungry with the mere thought of finding a handsome woman out in this wild country.

"Deke, even supposing she was good-looking," Tyler said, "she wouldn't be much to look at by now. She'd have shriveled up like a dried prune in this hot country.

She'd be skinny and dirty and her hair would be tangled with stickers and she'd have bruises and scrapes all over her body. She'd smell like goat and I'll bet she's a fright, even if she is still alive."

Deke scowled. "You sure know how to kill a man's idle daydreams."

"Let's ride," Modesto said, climbing heavily into the saddle. "We're going to fan out same as we did a couple days ago and keep looking for sign. We're going to find that girl, dead or alive."

"If she's dead, we'll never figure out where the mine is," Tyler said.

"They were a couple of tough sonsabitches," Modesto admitted with a grudging measure of respect, "I'll give 'em both that much. I never saw anyone that could stand up to the kind of beating we gave 'em and not break."

"I knew old George would go to his grave without sayin' nothin'," Tyler said, "but Ken would'a talked if he hadn't just up and died so sudden like."

"That sonofabitch!" Modesto cursed. "But at least we did find out that the mine is to the south and that the damn thing really exists."

"Fat lot of good that has done us so far. They must have hid their mine or else filled over the entrance with rock."

"I'll bet the girl can tell us where her father's mine can be found."

"I sure hope so," Tyler said. "Either that, or we're going to have to start robbin' stagecoaches or banks."

"Didn't do them other fellas much good," Modesto commented. "Two of 'em dead."

"But one is supposed to have gotten away."

Modesto spurred his weary horse into a shambling trot. "That's right and I'll bet he's got the girl right now and she's leadin' him to her father's mine."

"Or else he's puttin' the pork to 'er."

Modesto grinned. "Yeah, it's likely he's doin' that too."

"I seen that girl once in Carson City," Tyler said. "She's a good-lookin' gal and it'd be a real shame if she was dead."

"Well," Modesto said stubbornly, "if we don't find her pretty soon, she will be dead! So let's ride."

Amy Ross was riding Dan Smith, eyes glazed with pleasure, lips pulled back from her teeth and bare breasts heaving with each thrust that she took from the man inside of her.

Dan looked up at her and groaned, "We're going to kill each other if we don't finish this."

"Maybe," she panted, "but I can't think of a nicer . . . oh! Oh!"

Amy felt something hot and delicious explode inside of her and it sent shivers of pleasure racing to the tips of her toes and fingers. Her bottom jerked spasmodically and she collapsed on Dan, feeling him erupt with his own thunderous climax as his fingers sank into her surging buttocks. She hugged his neck and let him fill her once more.

Ten minutes later, they both climbed weakly off the bed and dressed. Amy looked over at Dan and said, "I hope this eases your disappointment in the mine."

"It does," he said. "No matter that I struck *borrasca* once again. Amy, you're my *real* pot of gold."

"We'll find another claim for you to work," she said, feeling a little shaky because of the hard and continuous lovemaking they'd been engaged in for most of the last week. Dan was right about that, they had to slow it down

94

a little but, so far, neither one could quite get their fill of the other.

"But first," Dan said, pulling on his boots, "we need to get you back to civilization and let everyone know that you're still alive."

"I'm particularly worried about my friends Jessie and Ki. They're probably sure that I'm dead."

"Then they'll be thrilled when we show up and prove you are very much alive."

"I've never been *more* alive, Doctor," she said, meaning it. "Can we leave for Austin tomorrow?"

"At daybreak," he promised. "If I had Biscuit . . . well, we could do it in one day. But without him, it'll take us two."

"Especially if we don't get some rest and behave ourselves," Amy said, coming over to place her hand on his shoulder. "Dan, did you really mean it when you said that we'd get married in Eureka?"

"I sure did," he replied. "I never thought I'd love again, but you proved me wrong."

"Am I so very different from your first wife?"

"No," he said, "in the most important ways, you two are very much alike. You're both beautiful."

"Says you," Amy laughed, loving the compliment even though she did not think of herself as very beautiful, especially not dressed in his baggy pants and shirt.

"You're beautiful to me. And you're strong and courageous," Dan said. "You are a real survivor, Amy."

Amy sighed. "Maybe we'll find Ken and that gold mine."

"Maybe," Dan said, "but I'm not counting on it."

"Me neither. And besides, it belongs to him, now that my father is dead. I'll expect no part of their discovery."

Dan stepped toward the door. "I'm going to finish stopping up the mine tunnel."

"Why?" she asked. "If it's *borrasca,* who cares if someone else came along and worked it?"

"If they struck it rich in my mine, I'd care plenty," he admitted. "And anyway, I'm going to drag Biscuit inside and then go up and start a landslide that will leave no trace that I was even here other than this cabin which will be dismantled by some old codger for the lumber and carted away, probably to be used in his mine for shoring."

When Dan went outside, Amy gave herself a bath using only a gallon of precious water and a rag. Even that little water could make her feel clean and refreshed again and Dan did not seem to begrudge her the luxury. Amy brushed her hair until it shone and then she went outside and helped Dan drag Biscuit's stiff little body a few yards inside the mine tunnel.

"I'd like to be alone with him for a minute," he said. "I'll be outside waiting."

Ten minutes later, Dan came out of the tunnel and Amy could see that he was extremely upset. It touched her to see how much a grown man could care for an ugly old burro, and Amy suspected that they had been together from the moment that Dan had first arrived in Nevada and gone off on his lonely odyssey of prospecting in this harsh and desolate country.

"It'll only take one stick of dynamite to touch off a landslide that will cover the mine's entrance," Dan said, taking one stick and leaving four more inside a watertight box.

"Just make sure that you have a long enough fuse to get down and out of harm's way," she warned him.

"I will," he promised. "And you need to get back to

the cabin. There won't be too much flying rock, but even a sliver could kill if it hit one of us in the head."

Amy went back to the cabin and stood by the front door. She watched Dan climb the steep hillside until he was about twenty feet above his mine and then she saw him carefully place the single stick of dynamite and wedge it in place between two large rocks. He then struck a match, waved to her and lit the fuse.

Amy held her breath as Dan jumped and slid down to level ground beside his mine, then came racing toward her. He was almost to the cabin when the powerful explosion went off like a bomb.

"Wow!" Dan shouted. "The man that sold me that dynamite said that it was packed extra strong and he wasn't just kidding!"

They both stared at huge cloud of dust that lifted over the mine tunnel and obscured it from view.

"It'll take a few minutes for all that dust to settle," Dan said, taking her arm and pulling her to his chest. "Amy, we might just as well go inside and find something pleasurable to occupy our time."

"I thought that we were supposed to start resting," she said, feeling her body respond to his touch.

"Tomorrow," he promised, hand snaking into her shirt and finding one of her lovely breasts, "tomorrow we'll show some self restraint."

Amy laughed and threw her head back as his lips found a sensuous hollow where her neck and shoulder melted together. She looked up at the sky and judged that the huge cloud of dust would be visible for perhaps a hundred miles.

★

Chapter 12

"Did you hear that!" Tyler shouted as their horses jumped with a start at the sound of the explosion.

"Of course I heard it!" Modesto shouted. "You think the rest of us are deaf, or something! And look!"

They all followed Modesto's finger in the direction of a huge mushroom cloud of rising dust. "Must be twenty, twenty-five miles away at least," Deke said. "Who do you suppose . . ."

"I don't know," Modesto interrupted, "but all of you mark the horizon well because we're going to see who is out there and what the hell they are up to."

"But what about the girl?" Tyler asked.

"Maybe whoever cut loose with that dynamite *has* the girl!" Modesto roared. "And maybe they found her father's mine and they're trying to cover or else open it up. Hell, I don't know but we're going to find out pretty damn quick!"

Modesto whipped his horse into a gallop. He suspected that the dust cloud would dissipate pretty quick and he wanted to make sure that they could find its origin. To do that, they needed to close the distance as quickly as possible. Sure, it was reaching for straws, but gawdammit, he was about to run out of patience and their horses were about run out—period!

By sundown, Modesto and his men were about where they thought that they had seen the rising cloud of dust originate. The light was getting poor in a hurry and each of the outlaws could feel their leader's sense of urgency.

"In another ten, fifteen minutes it's going to be dark," Tyler warned. "And we've got to find water for these horses before they plumb die on us!"

"We'll find water when we find out where that dust cloud came from," was Modesto's terse reply.

A quarter of an hour later, Modesto knew they could go no farther or they'd risk missing the explosion site altogether. "I saw some pines up a canyon yonder," he told his men. "Maybe we'll find water."

"We'd better," one of the men said, "or we might have to start out walking first thing in the morning."

Modesto shot the man a warning glance that told him he had best keep his fears to himself. Reining up the canyon, they rode up a well-worn game trail and found water within a mile. Their horses sank their muzzles in the little stream and took their fill, then sighed with contentment while their owners unsaddled them and turned them free to graze.

That night they all warmed salt pork and bread on sticks held over a campfire. Modesto was unusually quiet and that meant that he was in a very bad mood and no one should even ask him a question. Giving their leader a wide berth, the outlaws silently rolled into their blankets early and fell into a deep, dreamless sleep.

Modesto kicked them awake right after the sun began to inch over the eastern horizon.

"All right, get up and get movin'!" he roared. "We're going to find out who used dynamite and why they used it! And we're going to drink *their* damned coffee for breakfast."

The men piled out of the bedrolls and staggered, still half asleep, to catch up their horses. The animals had made an amazing recovery considering their earlier desperate condition. A night with fresh water and plenty of high-mountain meadow grass had also done wonders for their dispositions. In less than an hour, Modesto and his outlaws were out of the canyon and searching for the landmarks they had seen under the rising dust cloud about eighteen hours earlier.

Modesto was in the lead when they topped a low rise and saw the cabin. He jerked his horse up so cruelly that the animal actually reared in pain. Then, he sawed the horse around and spurred back over the rise and out of sight.

"Hold my horse," he said, jumping to the ground and grabbing for his binoculars. "This might prove to be exactly what we've been looking for."

"You think it's where she holed up?"

Modesto didn't answer as he hurried to the crest of the rise and then flattened on the ground. He raised the binoculars to his eyes just as a man and a woman emerged from the cabin. They held hands for a moment, then each of them shouldered a traveling pack.

"Jackpot!" he said with a cruel grin.

Modesto watched as the man and woman paused for

a moment and then he signaled for Tyler to hurry up and join him. When the man reached his side, Modesto pointed across the quarter mile distance between himself and the cabin.

"Is that the Ross woman?"

"Damned if I don't believe it is!" Tyler said, squinting into the bright sun. "I'm almost sure of it."

"Well, it's a young woman and we'll have a good look at her before long," Modesto said, winking lasciviously at his companion. "A *real* good look!"

Tyler wet his lips and grinned broadly. "You get her first, of course, but I want seconds."

"Fine," Modesto said. "But after I hump her, there ain't going to be a whole lot left to use."

"I'll take that kind of leavin's any time," Tyler said as they hurried back down to their horses.

"All right, boys," Modesto said. "We spotted a man and a woman down yonder and Tyler here *thinks* it might be George Ross's daughter. That being the case, we find out who the other fella is and then we make 'em show us the gold."

The outlaws brightened. One of them, Rafe Cowley, a lean, taciturn man with an ugly, knife-scarred face, said, "I figure they used that dynamite to cover up the old man's gold mine. Maybe they got as much as they wanted for now and plan to come back to it time and again."

"Maybe," Modesto said, jamming his boot into his stirrup and heaving his considerable bulk into the saddle, "and that's what we're going to find out."

"We going to kill the girl?" Deke asked, eyes dancing with excitement.

"Maybe you boys will want to screw her to death," Modesto said. "But we ain't doin' nothin' to her until we find her daddy's gold mine. After that . . . well, to the victors go the spoils."

The men laughed, something that they had not done in a good long time.

★

Chapter 13

Amy and Dan had not walked a hundred yards when the band of outlaws came boiling over a rise and raced down on them. Dan dropped his pack and struggled to lever a shell into his rifle.

"Amy, run for the cabin!" he shouted. "Run!"

Amy wouldn't run. Instead, she fumbled in her own pack for a six-gun, but both of them knew that they hadn't a prayer of winning and surviving a gun battle.

"Drop your weapons or we'll kill you!" Modesto bellowed at the top of his voice. "Drop 'em, I say!"

"What are we going to do!" Amy cried.

Dan shot a glance at their cabin. "They'd run us down before we could get to the cabin and even if we did make it, so what? I think we'd better try to talk our way out of this one. It's our only hope."

Dan lowered his rifle, then set the barrel down on the top of his boot. Amy moved as close to him as she could and she could feel her heart pounding. Who were these rough and terrible looking men? Would they shoot them down or . . . God forbid, try to take advantage of her?

Amy shivered. It was all that she could do to stifle a whimper and she was so frightened that her knees were actually shaking.

"You!" Modesto shouted. "Drop that rifle!"

Dan dropped the rifle and said, "They probably want whatever gold that they think I've found. After that, they may just let us go unharmed."

But even as Dan uttered those comforting words, he knew that they sounded hollow and false. So he steeled his nerve, threw his shoulders back and resolved to do whatever was necessary to save Amy.

The horsemen surrounded them and their leader, a large, brutish man dressed in black pants and a dirty white shirt with a black hat, dismounted and came over to face Amy.

"You're George Ross's daughter, aren't you!"

"Yes," she said.

"Where the hell is his gold mine?" Modesto demanded.

Before Amy could even think of a reply, the outlaw leader stabbed a stubby finger at the rock slide. "Did you cover it up yesterday with that explosion?"

"Yes," Dan said quickly. "We covered it up."

Amy looked at Dan with surprise but held her tongue. She did not know what Dan was up to and guessed that he wasn't sure himself, but she trusted his judgement.

"I'm askin' *you*," the big, coarse man snarled.

"Yes," Amy whispered. "We covered the mine up."

"But not before you took out a bunch of gold?" Modesto tore off their packs and shook them. He frowned and tossed the packs to his horsemen. "Find out how much gold they're packin' out."

The two horsemen emptied both packs, spilling their contents into the dirt.

"I found a couple of nuggets," one said. "Hell, ain't much, though."

Modesto's deepset eyes bored into them both. "How come you ain't packin' out more gold? You got it hid somewhere, don't you?"

"No," Dan said.

"Why not!"

Amy looked up and saw that Dan had run out of answers. "We . . . we were afraid of attracting attention. And . . . and we were going to Austin to buy a wagon and a team of horses, then take it out all in one load."

Modesto weighed this answer carefully. "And where were you headed with it?"

"To the Comstock Lode," Amy said. "We figured that there was so much gold and silver up there that no one would question us. It's also far enough away from my father's claim to keep anyone from coming here."

"Smart," Modesto said after a moment. "Real smart. How much gold is there in that mine?"

"Enough to make a hundred men rich," Dan answered without batting an eyelid. "There's a fortune buried in that hillside, but it isn't easy to reach. There's a lot of quartz in the rock formations and the vein of pure gold runs thin and rippling through the quartz."

The outlaws had dismounted and were hanging on every word. One of them said, "How come you only took out a couple hundred dollars' worth?"

"Like the lady said," Dan replied, "we were worried about raising suspicions."

"How deep is it covered?" Modesto asked, brow wrinkling. "How much rock has dropped over the damned mouth of the tunnel?"

"I don't know," Dan said.

Modesto's massive fist traveled only about four inches,

107

but when it hit Dan in the gut, the punch was so hard that it lifted him completely off his feet. His face went ashen and his eyes rolled up into his forehead and he collapsed to his knees.

Amy threw herself at the big man. Her hooked fingers raked at his eyes and even though she missed, she tore his left cheek open and would have tried to drive her thumb into his eye if he had not clubbed her with the back of his hand. When she didn't go down, Modesto hit her again, a looping swing that drove her to the ground with the taste of blood in her mouth.

"No!" Dan cried, falling forward and hanging onto Modesto for a moment before pushing away. "Don't hit her again!"

Modesto wasn't much taller, but because he was fifty pounds heavier he held all the cards in this game. Dan felt himself being lifted to the toes of his boots as the outlaw growled, "I'll kill you first, then the woman. I'll shoot you, but we'll screw her to death if you don't cooperate. You understand me?"

Dan nodded. He felt as if he were going to vomit and was having trouble getting his breath.

"Now," Modesto said in a voice so calm as to be all the more chilling. "How much rock are we going to have to move in order to get back into that gold mine?"

"Plenty," Dan gasped. "I didn't realize that the dynamite was packed so tight and had such a wallop. I must have dropped ten ton over the mouth of the tunnel."

"We ain't miners," Modesto hissed. "Just tell me how long it will take us to dig it out!"

"Two, three days. I swear no more!"

"You and the girl are going to start movin' rock," Modesto said, grinning wolfishly. "You're going to work like animals and you're going to tell us all about that beautiful vein of gold we're going to find inside."

Dan tore loose from the outlaw and he would have tried to knee him in the crotch and make a fight of it except for Amy, who was still on the ground, moaning. So, instead of swinging, he dropped to his knees and hugged Amy.

"It's going to be all right, darling. It's going to be fine."

The outlaws began to laugh, their voices strident and obscene. And deep in the marrow of his bones, Dan knew that nothing was ever going to be "all right" as long as they were at the mercy of these heartless killers.

"On your feet," Modesto hissed. "The both of you."

Dan helped Amy to her feet. There was no color in her cheeks and her eyes mirrored her fear. He pulled her close and then they were prodded back across the yard to the fresh landslide.

"Grab a pick, the both of you," Modesto ordered. "And get to work."

"This woman is in no shape to work."

Modesto had been smiling, but now his eyes slitted and his face turned as brittle and as cold as ice. "She'll either grab a pick or a shovel and work the face of that slide, or we'll take her into your cabin and she'll work on her back. Which is it going to be?"

"You sonofabitch!" Dan screamed, shaking with fury. "If I ever . . ."

His words died on his lips as Modesto pulled his gun, cocked back the hammer and placed the barrel right between his eyes. "You got anything more to say?" Modesto asked with a demented grin.

Dan couldn't find words so he dared to shake his head.

"I didn't think so. Now both of you, get to work."

"Come on," he said gently as he helped Amy move over to the face of the landslide. "Let's just do what the bad man says."

She looked sideways at him and nodded, her face pinched with pain. And then, together, they began to move rock with their bare hands.

★

Chapter 14

Jessie rode her dapple-gray mare north out of Austin. Before leaving, she had managed to find a pack burro and a man who had outfitted her for a two week trip into the harsh wilderness of Central Nevada.

"You be careful out there," he had warned. "There are outlaws and all manner of ornery men who'd like to kill you for that horse and your supplies and whatever else they could find on your person."

Jessie had patted a six-gun on her hip and knew that her Winchester carbine was loaded and ready. "If trouble comes my way, I'll be ready. I know how to hit what I aim for."

The outfitter had nodded but Jessie saw in his eyes that he was not convinced and thought that it was a bad mistake for a pretty young lady to be journeying off all by herself into the high desert.

The first night out of Austin, Jessie had camped near a small, marshy seep where she could get plenty of water for herself and her horse and the burro. She had slept fitfully, however, and now was back in the saddle even as the last morning stars were dying. Jessie knew the day would get hot and she made sure that both her canteens were filled as well as a skin waterbag that she carried for the horse and the burro. She rode through the morning picking her way northeast based on hunches and intuition.

At noon, Jessie saw a band of about a dozen wild mustangs galloping across a distant tabletop of land and she reined off in that direction because mustangs would not run in the heat unless either chased or spooked by man.

Ten minutes later, she saw a pair of horsemen following the mustangs and when they saw her they reined up and waved. Jessie galloped over to see them with the burro braying in protest.

One man was about twenty-five, handsome, and bold of eye. Beside him was an Indian or half-breed in his early teens.

"Well I'll be dingoed!" the man said. "Maybe I've finally gone over the edge and sit here dreaming I am seeing a beautiful woman out here alone."

"You're not dreaming," Jessie said, hardly in the mood to be flattered. "I'm alone but I'm looking for a friend."

"Damn," the mustanger said, thumbing back his hat. He was tall and lean, weathered the color of mahogany wood and had the whitest teeth Jessie had ever seen on a man. He said, "My name is Lance."

"My name is Jessica."

"And this here is Concho. He's half Paiute and half Spanish and as fine a mustanger as there is in Nevada, outside of myself, that is."

"I'm better than he is," Concho said. "I can *think* like a horse, but Lance just smells like one."

Lance threw back his head and laughed. "Ain't that boy some kind of joker, though. Ain't he!"

Despite the circumstances, Jessie had to smile at this good-natured pair. They were both riding extremely tall and handsome horses that Jessie knew carried a lot of Thoroughbred blood in their veins. Lance wore a six-gun, but neither man carried a rifle, probably because they were both traveling light enough to chase or simply wear down the mustangs.

"Handsome mare you have there," Lance said. "What is a lady like you doin' out here by herself?"

"I'm looking for another lady," Jessie said. "She's a friend of mine and disappeared when the stagecoach was held up a short while back."

"Didn't even hear about that," Lance said. "Concho and I have been out here catching and selling wild horses. Railroad buys and ships them off to the army posts. We get ten dollars for the best and five for them that aren't so good."

"I see," Jessie said. "I wonder if you've seen anyone else out here."

"You mean like your missing friend?"

"Yes."

Lance pulled down the brim of his hat. His face grew solemn. "We sure haven't, Jessica." He turned to the young Paiute. "Have you even seen any tracks?"

Concho nodded and pointed to the north. "Six horses. Two days ago."

"Well, why didn't you say something about it?" Lance asked.

"No money in saddle horses for us, Lance."

"Well," the mustanger said, "I reckon that's true enough. All the same, I sort of wished you said something."

"These tracks," Jessie said, "Concho, could you show them to me?"

"Sorry, miss, but I'm a mustanger, not a guide."

"We're partners," Lance said. "We made a team and one of us can't do a whole hell of a lot without the other."

"Then would you *both* take me to the tracks."

Lance studied Jessie for a moment and then he dismounted and sat down in the shade of his horse. "I guess we need to palaver a little while, miss."

Jessie started to argue about that but then Concho also dismounted and sat in the shade of his horse.

"All right," Jessie said, following suit as she sat cross-legged in the dirt and frowned. "I guess you want to know why it's so important to me to be out here searching for my friend and why I'd be interested in following those tracks you saw, Concho."

"That about sums it up," Lance said with a pleasant smile as he pulled out a sack of tobacco, some papers and rolled himself a cigarette. When he had his smoke going, he tossed the makings to Concho, who rolled one for himself.

"Miss Amy Ross has been a friend of mine for many years," Jessie began. "Her father, once a successful merchant, was bitten by gold fever and her brother contracted it as well. Anyway, they both came out here searching for a strike and we *think* they found one and were murdered because of it."

"You say you think they found gold, but you're not sure of it," Concho said, clearly confused on this point.

"That's right," Jessie told him.

114

"Then why would they want your friend?"

"Because they probably think she can lead them to the gold."

"Can she?" Lance asked.

Jessie decided to play her cards close to the vest. She didn't know these two men and, although they looked and gave the impression of being simple and honest mustangers, the prospect of a lost gold mine could and often did bring out the very worst in men. "I don't think so, but I can't be sure."

Lance and Concho exchanged glances. Lance finally said, "Miss Jessica, would you mind movin' your horse over yonder for a few minutes?"

Jessie took that as an invitation to leave them to talk. "All right," she said, "but first, I should tell you that I'll pay you fifty dollars each if you will lead me to the men that made those tracks."

"Even if they know nothing about your missing friend?" Concho asked.

"Yes, because I haven't anything else to go on," Jessie explained. "That many men might be part of the gang that wrecked the stagecoach. Maybe they have Amy."

"Maybe, but probably not," Lance said. "You willin' to gamble a hundred dollars?"

Not wanting to sound too eager or desperate, Jessie hesitated a moment, then finally nodded her head. "Yes."

"And you've got the money?"

"I . . . I do."

Lance clucked his tongue. "Lady, I'll give you this, you've got courage. Why, there's a lot of men in this country who'd just take advantage of you and then take your money, horse, saddle and the works."

"Let me show you both something," Jessie said, drawing her gun and cocking it in one smooth motion.

"You see that piece of quartz rock just up the trail?"

They turned and squinted into the sun. "Which one?"

Jessie fired and the quartz disintegrated into a thousand pieces. "That one."

"Pick another so I know it wasn't just luck," the mustanger requested.

Jessie picked another rock that was about the size of an apple. She aimed and fired in one smooth, unhurried motion and the quartz became dust.

"Satisfied that I won't be taken advantage of," Jessie challenged, "or do I need to shoot the horns off your saddles or some such foolishness?"

"Don't do that!" Concho exclaimed. "That isn't necessary, miss."

"Good," Jessie said, ejecting the two spent cartridges and replacing them with fresh ones. "Keep in mind that I'm better with that Winchester rifle than I am with a six-gun."

"We aren't likely to forget," Lance said, looking more than a little impressed. "So what happens if these six men whose tracks Concho saw *do* have your friend?"

"Then I'll have to figure out some way to rescue her," Jessie replied.

Concho snapped his fingers. "Just like that?"

"No, *not* just like that," Jessie said. "But I'll do whatever it takes to get Amy out of their grasp. I just pray that I'll have that problem."

Concho looked right into her eyes. "Meaning that she isn't already dead."

"Exactly."

Lance looked sideways at his young friend. "I've made up my mind, have you, Concho?"

"I have. Let's help her. The mustangs we were chasing can wait for another day. Besides, there wasn't more than half that we'd have gotten top dollar for. The rest were pretty scrubby and the Army might not have even taken them."

"Good enough," Lance said. He grinned and stuck his hand out.

Jessie took it and the mustanger's paw was as rough as the bark of a pine tree. "It's a deal."

"Sure is," he said, "and while I enjoy holding your hand, Miss Jessica, I really was stickin' my paw out for the money."

"Oh," she said, feeling a little foolish as she pulled her hand away and dug into her Levi's.

When they'd counted their money, Lance came to his feet and said, "Are you in a hurry?"

"A great hurry," Jessie replied.

"Then we'll have to unpack that burro, tie what we can to our horses and turn the little critter loose. He wouldn't last a half hour trying to keep pace with our horses."

"You're right," Jessie said. "And I suppose that he will do just fine out here by himself."

"There are whole bands of 'em running loose in this country," Concho assured her. "Prospectors turn them loose or they just escape to roam free. That old burro of yours looks as if he's earned his freedom."

"I couldn't agree more with you," Jessie said.

She unpacked her burro and then they divided up her provisions and personal things and tied them on their horses. That accomplished, Jessie turned the burro loose. For several long, confused moments, he just stood looking at them with a quizzical expression and then he turned and started to walk away, ears twitching back and forth.

Concho made as if he were going to catch the burro and that caused him to bolt and run, kicking his heels and braying as if he had pulled off some great escape.

"They're so smart that sometimes they even outsmart themselves," the half-breed said with a laugh. "That little fella will find himself some friends out here and he'll last at least a few winters before the coyotes or old age or disease drags him down."

"I hope so," Jessie said, watching the burro gallop stiffly over a hill.

"Let's ride," Lance said, jamming a boot into his stirrup and swinging gracefully into his saddle. "We've got a long way to go and maybe some hard catching up to do."

Jessie followed along behind and they turned north, starting out at a fast jog that Jessie knew could carry a horseman farther and faster than any other gait. She was extremely grateful for the strength and stamina of the dapple-gray mare she'd bought in Austin. She was not nearly as tall or as fast as either one of the mostly Thoroughbreds that she would follow for the next day or two, but the mare was in superb condition and Jesse knew that she would not quit or falter.

And even though Jessie had no evidence to support the hunch that the six horsemen whose tracks Concho had found had any ties to Amy, she felt almost certain that they did and she knew that this pair of mustangers would waste no time in proving that fact.

"Be alive, Amy," she whispered, "just be alive!"

★

Chapter 15

"What are we going to do when we get this mine open?" Amy whispered.

"I don't know," Dan confessed under his breath. "Right now, all we're doing is trying to buy a little time while we think of some way out of this miserable fix."

"I haven't come up with anything yet."

"Hey!" Modesto shouted. "Cut the talk and work faster or I'll cut your damned tongues out!"

Amy bit her lower lip and kept working as hard and as fast as she could. She knew that Modesto would never cut her tongue out because he thought that he needed her to find the alleged gold mine that her father was supposed to have found.

"Won't be much longer now," Tyler said, tipping a bottle of whiskey and gulping the liquor down. "I figure that they'll be into that gold mine before sundown."

"They'd better be," Deke growled. "I been a poor man all my life and that is about to end.

Dan had delayed the excavation work just as long as

he dared, but there wasn't any chance of holding back beyond a few more hours. That meant that the outlaws would discover that they'd been tricked and that would be the end of their patience. Feeling his pulse begin to race, Dan turned and wiped his dusty hands on his pants.

"All right," he said, not daring to look sideways at Amy. "It's time to tell you the truth. There's no gold mine here. Just a rock slide."

"What!" Modesto roared, stepping forward and grabbing him by the shirtfront.

"You heard me," Dan said, "we're digging for nothing. There's no mine. This is just another damned rock slide."

"The hell you say!" Modesto roared, drawing his six-gun.

"No," Amy cried pushing between them, "please don't kill him!"

"Step aside," Modesto ordered, cocking back the hammer of his pistol.

"I won't! And . . . and I'll never tell you where my father's gold mine is *really* hidden!"

Modesto glanced sideways at his men and Tyler said, "Maybe you'd better not kill 'em until we see if there really is a gold mine hidden under that rock."

"Other than to hide a paying gold mine, why the hell else would anyone cover it up!"

"Beats me," Tyler said.

"Me too," Modesto added. He pivoted around and slashed Dan across the crown of his head hard enough to drop him. When Amy tried to fight, he hit her too.

"Now you've gone and done it," Rafe said. "Let's quit pissing around and see if we really do have a mine or not."

The outlaws all jumped forward, bent, and began tossing rocks and shale between their legs.

"Jezus! What is that gawdawful smell!" one of them cried after about ten minutes of frantic excavation.

The other outlaws quickly recoiled as well, their faces twisting with disgust and revulsion.

"There's something big and *dead* in there! This ain't no mine shaft, it's a tomb!"

"Here," Modesto said as he angrily grabbed a shovel from one of the men. "Let me do it!"

Digging like crazy, Modesto quickly opened up the tunnel. He coughed and stepped inside but quickly retreated. "There's a dead burro inside! He buried a dead damned burro!"

The outlaws all exchanged disgusted glances, then they turned on Amy and Dan, who were cut and bleeding from the vicious pistol-whipping they'd just suffered.

Modesto raised his gun and said, "I'll kill you both if I don't get the truth this time."

"All right," Dan said, cradling his bleeding scalp. "This was my gold mining claim and it had nothing to do with her father. I worked it for months and we were just leaving."

"Why'd you waste a damn stick of dynamite to bury a burro!" Modesto demanded.

"I just . . . just thought a hell of a lot of Biscuit."

"Maybe," Deke said, "he really struck gold and killed the burro knowin' its stench would drive anyone away."

Modesto frowned, thinking about this. Finally, he said, "All right, let's drag the damned thing out and see for ourselves."

"I'm telling you the truth," Dan said with a grimace. "This mine is *borrasca*. There is little or no gold to be found inside."

"We'll be the judge of that," Modesto said. "And since that's your dead burro in there, drag the damned stinking thing out."

"I can't. It's too heavy."

"Help him!" Modesto ordered Amy.

She nodded and stepped forward. "I think we'd better do as they say and let them have a look into this mine."

Amy and Dan both held their breath as they staggered inside and then grabbed the dead animal. Together, they were able to drag its carcass out while the outlaws stood off to one side watching. The burro was stiff and bloated and it smelled terrible. When they had dragged its corpse off a ways, Modesto gestured toward the open shaft.

"All right, boys, find a lantern and get in there to look around for any sign of gold. Deke, you were a miner."

"Sure, but I never found much to speak of," Deke argued. "That's why I took up ridin' with you."

"Get a lantern and get the hell in there!"

Deke found a lantern and cautiously stepped inside, thumb and forefinger pinching his nose.

Modesto glared at the others. "Rafe, didn't you work in the mines a few years?"

"Uh-uh!"

"Worthless bunch of lazy bastards," Deke snarled.

Less than five minutes later, Deke popped out of the mine. "It's *borrasca* all right. Lot of quartz, but nothing to show for it."

"No gold?"

"Not a trace. Damned worthless hole is all he has here."

"I told you that," Dan said.

Modesto pivoted around and pinned his eyes on Amy, who was still dazed from the blow she'd taken, even though it had not been nearly as vicious as the one that he'd administered to Dan.

"All right, honey, for the last time, where is your father's mine?"

"It's south of here," Amy said.

"If you're lying, I'm going to make you wish you were never even born. I'm going to torture you until you scream bloody murder but first, I'm going to let all the boys have their fill of you. Is that understood?"

She nodded, too scared to speak.

"Good!" Modesto looked to his men. "Let's saddle up and ride out!"

"What about them?" Tyler asked. "What are they going to ride?"

"They can walk until they both drop," Modesto growled as he hurried away.

Chapter 16

"The tracks I saw," Concho said, standing up in his stirrups, "are just up ahead. Maybe a mile."

This was good news for Jessie. She had been fretting for days over Amy Ross's fate and knew that she would have no peace of mind until she found her friend.

"Jessie?"

She looked sideways at Lance. "What?"

"I just wanted to say that I hope you're not going to be too upset if these tracks have nothing to do with your missing friend. Could be almost anyone out here."

"I know that. But Concho did say that the horses were all shod and this is not cattle country so I suspect that the six riders were outlaws."

"Or soldiers," Lance said, "or maybe even mustangers like Concho and myself. This is a big, wide-open country, but there are all sorts of men crossing it for reasons of their own."

"We'll just find and then follow the track and see

where they lead. That's all we can do."

"That's right," Lance said.

Neither of them said anything more as they continued forward. Fifteen minutes later, they found the tracks.

"There are *two* sets," Concho said. "The ones I saw and then . . . the same bunch retracing themselves."

"And look," Lance said, jumping from his horse and kneeling in the dirt to trace the prints with his forefinger. "My, my," he said looking up at Jessie with a wide smile. "I think we've found your friend."

At those words, Jessie's heart almost stopped. She jumped down from her mare and hurried over to Lance's side. "What did you find!"

Concho joined them and then Lance said, "What we have here are footprints. Can you see them?"

The footprints were quite difficult to see because they had almost been obliterated by hoofprints. But as Lance moved along using his forefinger as a pointer, Jessie could see the footprints. After they had moved about a dozen yards, tracing each footprint, Lance stopped and beamed.

"Here you go, Jessie! This one is barely trampled at all. See how small it is? Probably about the size your own boot would leave."

Jessie planted her foot beside the print and measured. "You're right," she said, feeling a sense of elation. "This was either the track of a boy or a woman."

"But there's another print as well," Concho said, brow furrowing with concentration. "A man's footprint and he isn't wearing high-heeled riding boots."

"Yes," Lance said, "I'd noticed."

Jessie picked out the second set of footprints and after a moment, she looked at her two companions and said,

"You're the experts in this sort of thing. Give me your read."

Concho said, "What we have here is a man and a woman—or child—followed by a half dozen horses. And they're the same bunch whose tracks I saw moving north. Only now they're going mostly south."

"I can take a guess as to what has happened," Lance said, looking at Jessie. "Do you want to hear my theory, or would you rather make your own?"

"I have my own, but I'd like to hear yours as well," she told him.

"All right, here's what I think," Lance said turning back to the tracks. "I'd say that six men went north looking for a man and a woman. It was their tracks that Concho found. Later, they found a man and woman and took them captive. Now, they're driving them south. The only question is, why?"

"To find that gold mine," Jessie said. "I can think of no other good reason."

"It could be a posse returning a couple of escaped prisoners or wanted outlaws," Concho said.

"The Nevada State Penitentiary is in Carson City," Jessie pointed out. "If it were a posse, they'd be driving their prisoners westward instead of south."

"Yeah," Concho admitted, "I guess they would at that."

Jessie straightened and looked both north and south along the line of the tracks. "Would either of you care to guess the age of these fresher set of tracks?"

"I'd say two days," Lance replied. "Concho?"

"Less than that. Maybe eighteen hours."

Lance thumbed back his battered Stetson and regarded Jessie with his slate-gray blue eyes. "You're the boss,

Jessie. You make the call. Do we keep moving north and find out where this bunch grabbed their captives and try to figure out why, or do we turn and ride south and ride our butts off trying to catch up with 'em?"

"We've got to go south," Jessie said. "I say this even as I realize the risk, that this could all be a case of mistaken identity. That the horsemen have nothing to do with Amy and that the two on foot are just captured outlaws."

"That wouldn't explain the little footprint belonging to either a boy or a woman," Concho reminded.

"That's right," Jessie said, "it wouldn't. So let's ride south and try and overtake this bunch."

Jessie started for her horse but Lance called out to her.

"Hold up, now!"

"Is there a problem?" Jessie asked.

Lance hooked his thumbs into his gunbelt. "There might be."

"Then let's hear it."

"Well, Jessie, we agreed to lead you to the tracks of these six jaspers in return for fifty dollars each. We've done that."

"So?"

"So now getting tangled up with six outlaws. To my way of thinking," Lance said, "that is entirely another matter. It sure isn't worth getting shot over fifty dollars."

Jessie had to concede that Lance had a good point. "Do you want more money?"

"To risk our bacon," Lance said, "I'm afraid so. Concho and me don't look like much, but we still place a high value on our rough hides."

"How much value?"

"Another fifty dollars each and we'll lead you to the

128

bunch that you're after. But if you want us to try and help you rescue your friend, that's *really* going to cost you something."

Jessie arched her eyebrows. "Are you getting greedy and trying to take advantage of me?"

Lance assumed a pained expression. "Why, hell no! But when we catch up with them six, the odds will be two to one in their favor and that ain't real good. The men we are hunting aren't a pack of farmers riding out to the cornfield, you know. They'll be tough and if they have the taste of gold in their noses, they'll be willing to fight to the last drop of blood."

"You're right," Jessie said, unwilling to play down the risks that she was asking Lance and Concho to take up with her in order to save Amy. "It's going to be very dangerous work. There's a chance that we can rescue Amy without a gunfight, but that is not very likely."

"That's what I'm saying," Lance said.

"Then how much will it cost me to buy your guns?"

Lance looked sideways at Concho, who merely shrugged his shoulders. Lance scowled and said, "I don't know just yet. Why don't we just play this rope out awhile longer until we see what we've caught in the loop? If it looks like something we can throw and slap a brand on, then we'll talk money. But if these boys are too tough to handle and we all stand to get killed, then that is a horse of a different color."

"I see," Jessie said, unable to hide her disappointment.

"Lance," Concho said, "we can't just find them fellas and leave Jessie all alone with no way to help her friend. Not after taking a couple hundred dollars of her money."

Lance studied his younger friend. "That just doesn't set right with you, huh, Concho?"

"Nope. And I doubt that it does with you either."

"Yeah," Lance admitted. "I couldn't hardly walk away from that kind of situation."

Lance made a quick decision and extended his hand. "Jessie, give us another hundred dollars and we'll try to figure out some way to help you get your friend away from those outlaws."

"What about the other prisoner?" Jessie asked. "Any idea who he might be?"

"Not a one," Lance admitted. "And he's not going to be of any concern to us. We're signin' on to help Amy Ross, not some other yahoo who just happened to get himself into a fix. Is that clearly understood?"

"It is," Jessie said. "And now that we've come to terms, can we ride south?"

"As soon as you pay us another hundred," Lance said with that boyish grin of his that Jessie found quite irresistible.

That night they rode until almost midnight. The mustangers were tireless horsemen and their tall Thoroughbreds were in superb condition. Jessie's smaller dapple-gray mare was also in excellent condition, but the long, hard miles and the punishing afternoon heat were beginning to wear her down.

"I'm not sure that your mare is going to be able to hold to this kind of pace much longer," Lance said, watching Lady's head sink almost to her knees.

"We'll have to take it easier tomorrow," Jessie replied. "Because you're right about my mare. She strong and she's gallant, but she's not accustomed to the kind of country or the pace we are setting."

Although they were still many miles from the party they were trying to overtake, Lance decided that they should not risk a campfire.

"It'll be cold beef jerky and bread tonight," he said. "Got a little whiskey to wash it down with."

Jessie rummaged into her own pack and found several tins of peaches. "These will spice up the dinner a little," she said, taking one tin for each of them and going over to a rock where she would open them.

They ate with the sun going down and the air cooled off as soon as the last rays of the sun faded. Lance went over to check the hobbles on Jessie's mare saying, "Concho and I ride geldings but that dapple-gray of yours is pretty enticing bait for a wild mustang stallion."

"They'd risk coming in this close to our camp?"

"For a pretty female, a stud will risk almost anything," Lance said. "It ain't all that different with men, either."

Jessie felt her cheeks warm and he smiled and said, "I guess you must have men falling all over themselves when they're around you, huh, Jessie?"

"I'd be lying if I said that men didn't watch me."

"Yeah, I'd know better than to believe that," Lance said. "As a matter of fact, I have a pretty rough time keeping my own eyes off you."

"I take it you're not married?"

"I was once. For a couple of years, she even used to come out and help Concho and me mustang. But she got throwed and hurt one summer and then she gave it up. Busted her shoulder up and hurt her back."

"I'm sorry to hear that."

"Me too." Lance sat down on a rock as the first stars begin to appear. "I got blamed for that, of course. She began to harp on me every day about finding a new line of work. She wanted me to settle down in some city job.

She used to talk about me opening a livery, or a saddle shop."

"Maybe you would have been good at that," Jessie said.

"Not likely," Lance replied with a gentle shake of his head. "You see, I can't read nor write. Figures other than what I expect to get paid for selling a horse just naturally confound me. Anyway, about a year later, my wife ran off and left me with a traveling writer who was heading back to Boston and agreed to take her along if she would bunk up in his sleeping car for the whole trip."

"I'm sorry," Jessie said, reading pain in the man's eyes. "Life can often be cruel."

Lance was quiet for a minute, then he said, "Sure it can. And the good don't always overcome the bad. Whatever justice there is sure doesn't enter into what happens in life."

"I'm not sure that's true," Jessie said. "Life is unfair and a mystery, but it seems to have an order."

"Not as far as I can see," Lance said. "But I do know this, Miss Jessie. There is not much in life that confounds you. And I'll bet that you could open damn near any kind of business and make it a success."

"I was brought up by my father playing with numbers and ledgers instead of dolls," Jessie told the mustanger. "My father was an extremely successful entrepreneur and a first-rate businessman. He probably wanted a son to carry on his legacy of an international fortune. Obviously, he got a girl and he decided to make the best of it and teach me accounting, finance and investments. So, to answer your question, business and finance do not worry me."

"Yeah," Lance said, "I could tell you was a big deal

132

from the minute I laid eyes on you. Some women, they dress up real nice and put on airs. But the ones that dress nice without any fuss or talk, now they're the ones that really have the money."

"Does money mean a lot to you?" Jessie asked, genuinely curious about this man.

"Money means that I have enough in my pocket to outfit another mustang hunt," Lance told her. "I love this country and the freedom that mustanging has for me. The truth of the matter is that I can ride for twenty hours straight and never get tired of seeing the country. It's always changing and Nevada is legendary for its wild mustangs. The big game hunters sometimes come and want me to help them mustang, but I won't do it."

"Why not?"

"There are some things that money can't buy. I won't sell out to some rich man so he can shoot a wild stallion, then maybe have its head mounted and sent back east to be nailed to his office or library wall."

"I admire that," Jessie said. "Most men would just sell out and take the money."

"Not me and not Concho."

"When we find those men," Jessie said, "and if Amy is with them, I want you to know that I won't hold you to anything."

Lance cocked an eyebrow at her. "Meaning?"

"Meaning I won't expect you to risk your life."

"I see. But you will."

"Yes," Jessie told him. "But that is different because Amy is my friend."

"I understand that," Lance said. "But there is a matter of honor here that we need to discuss. You see, Concho and I do have our standards."

"I know but . . ."

133

"And leaving two pretty women to try and outwit, outrun, or outfight six outlaws just wouldn't be in keeping with those standards."

"So you will fight, if it comes down to that."

"I reckon."

Jessie reached out and touched Lance and before she knew it, he was pulling her into his arms, his mouth on her mouth, his hands running over her body.

"No," she whispered as he pushed her back onto the earth and began to unbutton her blouse. "Lance, we can't . . ."

Jessie gasped with pleasure as his tongue tickled her nipple and slid wetly across her breast. Whatever it was that she was about to tell him they could not do was instantly forgotten, and when he began to pull off her riding skirt, she closed her eyes and relaxed, knowing that this big, rough man was going to feel hard and even violent but that she would enjoy his frenzied lovemaking.

Jessie was not disappointed. He took her much as a wild stallion would take a mare in heat. He mounted her and his big rod slammed into her womanhood. Jessie bit her lower lip and felt him thrusting powerfully. She spread her legs wider and felt one of his hands cup her buttocks. In moments, her juices turned sharp discomfort into extreme pleasure. He felt huge inside her body and both smelled and felt like a stallion as he pounded her into a state of intense desire.

Jessie clung to him. Tightened herself and then she locked her legs around his waist and made him slow his ride. The stars began to appear and he kept riding her until she was bucking like a filly and biting his neck, his throat, his ear and pleading with him to finish with her before she was so bruised and used that she could not

134

take up their chase early in the morning.

"Did you like it?" he asked her after the second time he took her that night and while they were heading back to join Concho at their campfire.

"Yes," she confessed, "I liked it. And you?"

"The best," he said, grinning broadly. "Even better than I'd been picturing in my mind."

"Good," she told him. "Now let me sleep so that I will be able to ride tomorrow."

"Fair enough," he said. "But I'll make no promises tomorrow night."

Jessie was hoping to overtake the six outlaws and free Amy by tomorrow night. But there seemed to be no point in telling him that for the time being.

"Get lost out there in the dark?" Concho asked trying to stifle a grin.

"I guess we did," Lance said. "Did you get lonely sitting here all by yourself?"

"I guess that I did," Concho said. "But I had a useful thought while you two were off star-gazing."

"What thought?" Jessie asked.

"I was thinking that there was this prospector. A nice fella named Dan and he was working a claim just north of here. He was real secretive about it about it but several Indians told me that he used to treat their people with the white man's medicine. Could be that he was the man that they captured along with your friend, Jessie."

"But why?"

"I couldn't say, but he was the only one that I know for sure used to work this area. I'm told he had a gold mine somewhere just to the north."

"It's a possibility," Jessie said. "It would explain Amy's disappearance."

"But what would the outlaws want with a doctor?"

"Maybe one of them has been shot," Concho said. "Or maybe they just figure this fella is gives them some good insurance in case there is trouble."

"Or," Jessie added, "Amy simply refused to do anything unless this man who saved her was allowed to live."

"It could," Lance agreed, "be any or none of those reasons. The main thing is that it appears that there are two hostages and they're being forced to march south."

"Poor Amy," Jessie fretted out loud. "I can only imagine how awful it must be to have to march under the guns of those outlaws who are probably the very same ones that killed both her father and her brother."

There was a long silence and then Lance said, "We'll try to catch up with them tomorrow. Maybe get into their camp tomorrow night under the cover of darkness. We'll figure out a way, Jessie. Just quit worrying and try to get some rest."

Jessie nodded, appreciating his concern. She *was* extremely tired but, if her mare were up to the mark, Jessie would have ridden all night in order to reach Amy a few hours sooner.

★

Chapter 17

"Look!" Concho said. "See that plume of rising dust?"

Jessie shielded her eyes to the glare of the sun. Perhaps five miles to the south she saw a thin, almost invisible wisp of dust on the horizon. "Concho, how do you know it's not just a dust devil?"

"Not the right shape."

"Or," Jessie added, "mustangs?"

"Still not the right shape," the half-breed repeated.

"What he means," Lance said, choosing to elaborate, "is that mustangs don't raise dust unless they are chased. And the dust cloud you are looking at wasn't caused by a band of wild horses. If we been mustanging long enough to know that."

"Then what?" Jessie asked.

"I don't know," Lance said, "but we ought to be finding out within the next hour."

"Do you think it's them?"

"Damn good possibility," the mustanger said. "My guess is that they've stopped someplace, probably where

137

they think George Ross had his gold mine. There are quite a few abandoned mines in this country. Some of the tunnels go in just a few feet, others are very deep."

"I see." Jessie mopped her brow. The sun had been unmerciful this day and she would certainly welcome sundown. "Well, let's find out."

Lance and Concho checked their six-guns and Jessie could tell that they were also both very anxious to overtake the band of outlaws.

"The timing is good," Concho said, "because we ought to be there about an hour after dark."

"Yep," Lance agreed. "And then, all we have to do is wait until they fall asleep, free the girl, and make tracks."

"And steal their horses," Concho said. "Otherwise, they would run us down because our own animals are so played out."

"Good point," Lance said in full agreement. "The plan makes sense to me. What about you, Jessie?"

"I want to arrest them," she heard herself tell Lance. *"Arrest 'em!"*

"That's right," Jessie said firmly. "If they are connected to the deaths of George and Ken Ross, they need to go to trial. And, if that isn't enough, they ought to spend a long time in prison for kidnapping Amy and whatever luckless soul that they have also taken captive."

"Now just a minute," Lance protested. "Sneaking into their camp and freeing up your friend is one thing, arresting six hardcases and getting them back to a courtroom to stand trial is quite another."

"I agree," Jessie said. "It will be more difficult. But it has to be done."

"Shit," Concho swore. "We're probably going to get killed tonight."

"Don't be such a pessimist," Jessie snapped. "We'll catch them sleeping and disarm them before they even know what is happening. I don't see any reason for great concern."

"Oh you don't, do you?" Lance challenged.

"No, I don't."

Lance looked over at Concho, who rolled his eyes. Without further conversation, the two mustangers spurred their horses forward and Jessie followed. Her mare was so exhausted that the poor animal was almost staggering.

"Not much farther now," Jessie told the weary animal. "Not much farther at all."

Darkness dropped like a black shroud over the land and a thin moon hung suspended over the high Nevada desert. Somewhere out in the night, a pack of coyotes howled, their lonesome cries sounding faint and mournful. Jessie saw Concho rein his horse up sharply and then saw him lean forward in his saddle like a dog sniffing the wind.

"They're less than a mile ahead now," Concho said after several long moments. "Can you smell their campfire?"

"Nope," Lance said. He twisted in his saddle toward Jessie. "Can you?"

"No," she said after a moment.

"They are roasting sage hen," Concho said. "If we hurry, we might be invited to eat dinner."

Lance scoffed. "The only thing we'd be invited to eat is their bullets."

"We'd better leave the horses here and go ahead on foot," Lance said as he dismounted and tied his reins to a piece of sage. "Just don't loosen your cinch, Jessie, because we may be leaving in a hell of a big hurry."

Jessie understood. She dismounted and tied her mare,

139

who looked to be too tired to go anywhere. Taking her Winchester from its saddle scabbard, Jessie nodded to indicate to the men that she was ready.

"No noise," Concho warned.

"Shut up," Lance replied.

Jessie followed the two mustangers into the sage and, despite her own physical weariness, it felt good to be walking. They went single file. Concho, who seemed to have the keenest sense among the three of them, was in the lead. The idea that she would soon be seeing Amy again filled Jessie with a great deal of excitement and she prayed that everything would turn out all right.

After a half hour, Concho slowed their pace and now Jessie could smell the cooking sage hen. It did smell wonderful and it reminded her that they had not had anything to eat since morning and that had only been a few hard biscuits. A few moments later, she heard voices and she followed Concho and Lance's example by crouching and moving very slowly.

Concho dropped to his knees and raised his hand in signal. He began to crawl forward toward firelight that Jessie could now see through the brush. What seemed to take hours probably did not take more than five minutes but, at last, they came to the outskirts of the firelight and flattened on the ground to study their quarry.

Jessie saw Amy immediately. It was all that she could do not to jump up and charge forward with her six-gun blazing in order to rescue her friend, who appeared to be in bad shape. Amy and what must have been Dan were roped together back-to-back. They were sitting apart from the outlaws and their hands had been untied so that they could eat the scraps of meat that were being tossed to them by the six outlaws. It was a cruel sight for Jessie and she could see the suffering that her friend had endured from these heartless men.

"Tomorrow," one of the outlaws warned, "we either find gold in your father's mine or else I'm sending you both on a one-way trip to the promised land. You understand me, Dan?"

Dan looked up and Jessie could see the defiance in his face and she was filled with pride when she overheard him say, "Sooner or later, you'll be joining us."

The outlaw jumped to his feet, face red with anger. He placed his hand on his six-gun and shouted, "I swear you'll both die slow if we don't find that vein of gold! I tell you, we're tired of foolin' around with this thing!"

"My father's mine runs deep into that hillside," Amy said in a shrill voice. "We only just got here this morning. Do you think he'd have just left the vein of gold exposed and gone away? Of course not! He covered it up and it's going to take some hunting to find it."

"You got until tomorrow," the leader of the outlaws said. "No gold by sundown, we're going to have a fine time amusing ourselves with you tomorrow night."

Jessie was seized by a fit of rage. It was all that she could do not to simply come to her feet and shoot the big outlaw down in cold blood and then turn her gun on the others. But a shred of reason held her in check. Jessie knew that she and her friends stood little or no chance of surviving a full-blown gun battle with the six dangerous and seasoned looking outlaws.

Lance reached out and touched Jessie's arm. He forced a smile and then rolled over onto his back and closed his eyes to rest. Concho did the same.

Yes, Jessie thought, the thing to do is to calm ourselves and wait until those men are all asleep, then make our move. If they could free Dan and Amy and get guns into their hands, the odds would then be four against six and

141

they'd have the element of surprise.

Jessie rolled onto her back and gazed up at the heavens. After just a few minutes, she saw a shooting star blaze across the sky and she took that as a good omen. And then, despite the gravity of their situation, she closed her eyes and allowed her deep physical exhaustion to carry her off to sleep.

★

Chapter 18

Lance took a deep breath. "It appears to me that they're all asleep. Concho, you go after their horses while Jessie and I free Amy and her friend. Once that's accomplished, we can try and disarm them fellas and put them under arrest."

"I don't think that will happen," Concho said, "it'd be like trying to defang a den of rattlesnakes in the dark."

"We have to try," Jessie said. "These men are stagecoach robbers and murderers. I'm not about to just let them get away with their crimes."

"Whatever you say," Concho said, for he was in no mood to argue. "But if all hell breaks loose, I want you to know that I'll have their horses untied and I'll be waiting for you on the other side of their camp, down near that arroyo."

"Got it," Lance said. "If this goes sour, we'll come to you and leave these boys stranded out here. Maybe we could even go and get some reinforcements."

"Maybe so," Concho said a moment before he set off to flank the camp.

"If anything happens to Concho," Jessie whispered, "I'm going to feel responsible."

"What if I get killed?" Lance asked, sounding hurt. "Ain't you going to grieve a little over me too?"

He was teasing and it broke the tension. "Yes," Jessie said, mustering up a smile, "I'll grieve over you as well."

"Well, at least that's something," he said, trying to sound only slightly mollified. "But Jessie, this is serious. If I go down for keeps and things go bad for our side, I want you to promise me you'll get to Concho and those horses. When you do, ride for your life. You see, those men don't need another pretty woman to mistreat and you can't help your friend if you're taken captive. Agree?"

"Agreed," Jessie replied. "But I'm confident that we can do this whole thing without a shot being fired, at least, not by them."

"You are some kind of lovely daydreamer," he said, checking his six-gun. "Let's go!"

Jessie rose to her feet beside Lance and they started toward the camp in a crouched position, guns up and ready. As they closed on the outlaws, Jessie could hear her heart pounding and over that, the sound of heavy snoring. This was, she felt very sure, going to work.

Lance and Jessie had both agreed to head for the tree where Dan and Amy were tied. Once the pair were freed, they could begin to disarm the outlaws. There would be four of them and it should go quickly.

When Jessie reached her friend, Amy's chin was resting on her chest and she was sleeping fitfully. Up close and even though bathed in the weak moonlight,

Amy looked so thin and haggard that Jessie scarcely would have recognized her friend under ordinary circumstances.

Lance knelt in front of Dan and together, just as they'd rehearsed, they both clamped their right hands over the mouths of Amy and Dan to prevent them from crying out in surprise.

It worked. Amy was so startled that she attempted to scream and Dan made a muffled sound of surprise, but once they gained their wits, both of them froze and stared.

"It's all right," Jessie whispered, feeling her eyes sting with salty tears. "Amy, we're going to get you and your friend out of this mess right now."

Lance had a sharp knife and it took him only a moment to cut the ropes that bound the pair of captives. To his credit, Dan did not ask any foolish questions but accepted the situation as it was and then offered to help.

"Just tell us what you want us to do," he said in a low voice. "We're willing to help you kill them, if necessary."

"Hopin' it won't be," Lance said. "We're going to try and disarm 'em while they're sleepin'."

"And then?"

"Then we'll wake 'em all up and see if they want to cooperate or feed the coyotes," Lance said matter-of-factly.

"Do you have a gun I can use?" Dan asked.

"Not yet," Jessie said, motioning toward the sleeping outlaws, "but we hope to solve that little problem right now. Can you move or are you too stiff?"

"I can move," Dan said.

"We've been tied up since noon, but I'll try," Amy said. "Jessie, however did you find us!"

"I'll tell you later."

"Yeah," Lance agreed, "this isn't the time or the place to chew the fat."

"Let's go!" Jessie whispered with urgency.

But Dan and Amy could barely stand. The rope that had bound them together had been so tight it had cut off the circulation to their legs, and they both almost collapsed.

"I think," Lance said, "that we'd better get them mounted on horses and come back alone."

Jessie nodded. "I agree."

"But I want to help!" Dan whispered urgently.

"The best thing you can do is to be on a fast horse just in case things go to hell in a hurry," Jessie explained. "Same for you, Amy. Now please don't argue. There is no time."

They both wanted to argue but when they took another step and found that they could not stand without support, much less sneak in among the outlaws to disarm them, Dan and Amy readily agreed to do as Jessie thought best.

Concho had the horses untied and since the outlaws had pitched their tack near their rope corral, it only made good sense to saddle and bridle all six animals.

"We can sell the saddles and bridles just as easy as the horses," the half-breed explained.

"Give me a hand," Lance said, half-carrying Dan over to one of the horses that Concho already had saddled. "These two were tied up so tight that they don't have any circulation in their feet or legs. Might take an hour or so to get their blood circulating again."

"I'll never be able to repay you men for this," Dan said, his voice thick with emotion, "unless, that is, I finally strike it rich."

"We won't hold our breath," Lance said as they heaved Dan into the saddle and gave him the reins.

"What am I supposed to do?"

"Not a damned thing except stay out of the way," Lance said.

Amy was the next to be lifted onto a horse and when all the outlaw mounts were saddled and bridled, Lance, Concho and Jessie started back toward the camp prepared to do whatever was necessary in order to capture the outlaws.

They moved as silently as shadows among the sleeping figures, looking for the outlaws' weapons. A couple of the outlaws had removed their gunbelts and laid them by their sides, but most of the wary men were sleeping with six-guns tucked under their blankets or belts.

The leader of the gang was one of those men who had not removed his Colt. Jessie bent over the big man and took a deep breath. She placed her hand on the outlaw's gunbutt and slowly began to extract it.

Modesto was awake in an instant and his hand batted Jessie's gun aside and crashed against the side of her jaw. Reflexes caused Jessie's trigger finger to jerk and her gun emptied a harmless bullet into the night sky.

Jessie struggled to remain conscious. She could hear shouts and gunshots. Amy screamed and Jessie heard horses thundering through the camp which was in a state of confusion and chaos. Jessie struggled to react, but she was dazed and helpless. A man's body struck the ground close to her and when Jessie tried to climb to her feet, someone fired a pistol at almost pointblank range beside her ear and then clubbed her to the earth. After that, everything lost focus and meaning.

Lance tried to reach Jessie but Modesto grabbed and used her as a shield while his gun bucked in his big fist. Lance took three slugs and tumbled into an ocean of pain. Lance heard Concho yell something as he tried to climb back to his feet, but Modesto shot him again and his body went stiff a moment before it relaxed in death.

Concho gunned down a man but also took a bullet that shattered his forearm completely. He threw himself to the ground as more bullets probed for him like dark fingers of death. Gripped by fear, Concho scuttled back into the brush hearing Dan and Amy shouting. Concho knew that the pair had no weapons and that their only hope was to escape taking all the outlaw horses with them.

"Run!" he yelled into the night as he also tried to escape, hearing the outlaws shouting and cursing.

Concho knew that Amy and Dan would never find him in the dark. His only hope of escape was to reach the two Thoroughbreds and the dapple-gray mare that Jessie had ridden. If he could do that, he had a chance.

Concho did not have the capacity of tears but he was devastated by grief. Despite all their careful planning, nothing had gone right back at the outlaw camp. He had seen Lance take at least three bullets and he knew that his mustanging partner was dead. There was nothing that could be done about that now. And as for Jessie, well, Concho did not want to think about her fate. Maybe, if she was lucky, she had also been shot and killed in that first murderous volley.

Concho's arm was numb and he knew that he was bleeding heavily. He tore off his bandana and tied it around his forearm, grunting with pain. He tightened the bandana using one hand and his teeth. And then, he climbed to his feet and began to run to get their horses.

There was no hope of victory anymore. Sure, they'd

killed two, maybe even three of the outlaws. But Lance was dead and Jessie ought to be. All in all, it had been a bloody and a terrible night.

It seemed to Concho as if he had to run forever before he finally reached their horses. He did not know if the outlaws were hot on his heels or not and had no intention of waiting around to find out. He did not know if Dan and Amy had possessed the presence of mind to take out outlaw horses when they'd fled during those few moments of death and utter confusion. Most likely, they had not.

Concho hauled himself onto his tall horse and gathered the reins of the animals belonging to Lance and Jessie.

"Come on!" he said, urging the weary animals into a heavy gallop. "We've got to find Jessie's friends before the outlaws find them and get their horses back!"

★

Chapter 19

Concho caught up with Amy and Dan, neither one of whom was any great shakes on horseback. Weak and battered by their grueling ordeal, they clung to their saddlehorns and it would not have surprised Concho had they simply toppled sideways off their running horses and broken their necks.

"What about the other horses!" Concho screamed as he raced in and dragged their horses to a stop. "What happened to the outlaws' other four horses!"

Amy appeared to be in shock. She twisted around in her saddle and stared back through the inky darkness. "What happened to Jessie!"

"I don't know," Concho said. "The last I saw she was alive."

"And the other man?"

Concho shook his head, not trusting himself to speak about Lance and how he'd died in a hail of gunfire.

"Oh damn!" Amy whispered. "We gained nothing! We just traded Jessie and that other man for Dan and

151

myself! Better we'd have died than this!"

Concho secretly agreed. He would much rather have had Lance and Jessie survive than this pair of pathetic strangers. And to make matters worse, if the surviving outlaws managed to get a hold of those four loose horses, they would probably decide to come hunting for their escaped prisoners.

"Shall we go back?" Dan asked.

"No," Concho said. "My friend is dead and Jessie . . . well, she wouldn't want the three of us to die on her account."

"I *won't* abandon her!" Amy cried, trying to drag her horse around and go back.

But Concho knew that to return would be to die. And if they died, then that would mean that Lance had died for nothing. Concho knew that he could not allow that to happen so he tore the reins from Amy's hands.

"We're going to reach Austin come hell or high water," he vowed. "And to do that, we're going to have to ride and hide like Apache. We're not out of this yet. The outlaws may decide to come after us and, frankly, they'll catch us if we don't ride like the devil was nipping at our heels."

"He's right," Dan said. "Amy, we're not even armed."

"But they've got Jessie!"

"If she's dead," Concho said, "then there is nothing that we can do for her. And, if she still alive, there's still nothing we can do for her. Either way, we have to try and reach Austin alive. Maybe we can find help."

"There's not even any law there!"

"I know," Concho said. "But we can ask for volunteers to form a posse."

Dan nodded but he did not look very hopeful of that possibility and Concho could well understand why. As far as Concho was concerned, Jessie was already as good as dead.

Jessie wasn't sure how long she had been unconscious, but she thought less than an hour. She awoke when the outlaw leader poured water onto her face from his canteen and then kicked her in the ribs.

"Wake up!" he ordered.

Jessie moaned. Her head felt as if it were being split like firewood.

"Who the hell are you!" Modesto demanded. "And who were them other ones that stole our horses!"

Jessie spluttered and managed to sit erect. "We're friends of the two that you held captive. We were just trying to free them. We hoped to escape before you awakened tomorrow morning."

"You gunned down two of my men!" Modesto hissed. "You wounded two others! And worst of all, the girl escaped and we still ain't found her daddy's gawddamn gold!"

Jessie tried to shake the fuzziness from her mind. She took a couple of deep breaths and realized that there were four of them surrounding her and they all looked ready to kill.

"Let's screw her 'til she screams and then cut her throat," one of the men said. "On account of her, Tyler and Mace are dead and I got a bullet hole in my damned leg!"

Jessie turned to the man. "If you kill me, you'll never find that Ross gold mine and everything you've done so far will have been a big waste of time."

"You know where the gold mine is?"

"Not exactly," Jessie hedged, unsure of what Amy had told them and afraid she might get crossed up with conflicting stories. "But I do know it's still farther to the south."

"And just how do you know that?"

Jessie told them about how she'd figured out the approximate location of the hidden gold mine. She ended up by saying, "There's a couple other little things that you need to know that will help to find it, but I'm not stupid enough to tell you everything."

Modesto reached out and grabbed Jessie by the throat. She curled her fingers and raked his cheek, furrowing the flesh under her nails and taking satisfaction in seeing her slashes fill and then run with blood.

Modesto howled and drew back his fist to bash her in the face. Jessie saw the blow coming and tried to duck, but he had her by the throat so that she could not even turn her head. After that, she tumbled back into the absolute darkness.

When Jessie awoke the second time, her right eye was swollen almost completely closed. She was riding behind the outlaw leader and her hands were tied to the latigo strings so that she could not move them even an inch.

"Where are we?"

"We're going to find that gold mine," Modesto vowed. "And if we don't find it, we're going to get rich anyway."

"How?"

"Well, *Miss Jessica Starbuck*, we're going to hold you for ransom since you're so rich and important."

"How did you find out?"

"You kept your receipt for the train ride you took on the Union Pacific Railroad. Now, I wouldn't have paid it any mind except that was marked as a *first-class ticket*. I never even knew anyone to travel first class, much less

154

do it myself. But after we find the Ross gold mine or collect a bounty on your pretty ass, me and the boys are going to travel first class for the rest of our lives."

"Then you won't be traveling very far or very long," Jessie said, "because your days are numbered."

"Talk is cheap," one of the outlaws sneered. "As far as we've got it figured, either way, we're about to cash in on a big payday."

"You figure wrong when it comes to ransoming me," Jessie said. "And as for the Ross gold mine, well, that's no guarantee either."

"We'll see," Modesto said. "I'm a man that likes to play his gut hunches because they're almost always right. And my hunches tell me that we're going to be rich."

"Your hunches are about to bring you down," Jessie said.

Modesto's hand dropped to Jessie's thigh and his thick fingers bit into her flesh so hard that she paled but somehow managed not to cry out in pain.

"Either way, Miss Starbuck," Modesto said, "we're going to get real well acquainted. Real well."

"Over my dead body."

Modesto chucked obscenely. "Now that," he said, "might not be so bad either."

Jessie wanted to throw up all over the man's back. The sun was blazing and she felt weak and dizzy. She needed water, food and rest, in that order. But first, she needed to figure out a way to escape before Modesto and his filthy friends found the time to repeatedly rape her.

"Did they get away?" she asked after a long silence.

"You mean that other woman and the fella we had tied up?"

"Yes."

155

"Hell no! We killed them all. Didn't mean to kill the girl, but the light was so poor that she went down riddled as bad as the others."

"You're lying."

"I'm not!" Modesto looked to his friends. "Ain't that right, boys? Didn't we gun down Amy Ross and all three of the men?"

The outlaws nodded their heads. And, for the briefest of moments, Jessie actually fell for their lie. Tears filled her eyes and she would have scrubbed them away if her hands had not been tied to the saddle.

To her shame, the outlaws saw a tear slide down her cheek and they began to hoot with derision. Right then, Jessie knew that she would never try again to bring these men to justice but would shoot them to death given her very first opportunity, if one ever came her way.

"Say," Modesto called back over his shoulder. "Who was you traveling with on the Union Pacific Railroad?"

"None of your business."

"Your husband? Are you married? If you are, shall we write and tell your old man what a good screw you gave the whole damned bunch of us? Or was it that Chinaman that Tyler shot down in front of the hotel?"

"You were behind that?"

"That's right. Your friend was asking questions that he shouldn't have been asking. We happened to be in town and decided we might as well take care of him so that he didn't cause us any harm later. I told him my name was Steve Hanson and the fool actually seemed to believe me!"

Modesto began to laugh and the other outlaws hooted with mirth. They were enjoying themselves, laughing and making vile and disgusting talk and obscene gestures in an attempt to reduce her to a state of hoplessness.

"I hope that you are laughing when the man you failed to kill comes to send you to hell."

"*Who* means to send us to hell!"

"Ki!" she heard herself blurt. "He's my friend and protector. He'll find and kill you one by one."

"Ki?" Modesto said in a mocking voice. "What kind of a damned name is that?"

"He's a samurai," Jessie said. "You won't even see him coming until you are on your way to the grave."

Jessie's dire prediction sent the outlaws into gales of laughter. Let them laugh, Jessie thought, because Ki will send them howling into the depths of hell.

★

Chapter 20

Concho, Amy, and Dan arrived at Austin two days later. Amy and Dan were clinging to their saddles, more dead than alive when they were carried into the hotel. Fortunately, Dr. Alton was over from Eureka and he took charge of the pair. Once Concho knew that the pair were being cared for, he asked, "Where can I find the man named Ki?"

"You mean that Oriental fella that was ambushed in front of this hotel?"

"That's right."

"He's staying upstairs. Second room on the right. The doc was planning to take him over to Eureka tomorrow."

Concho hurried up the stairs and when he came to the samurai's room, he knocked. There was a long pause and then the samurai said, "Who is it?"

"A friend of Jessica Starbuck. She's either dead, or in real big trouble."

The door flew open but Concho saw no one until he stepped inside and then felt a knife pressed to his kidney.

"Hey," he exclaimed, "I said that I was a friend!"

Ki removed the mustanger's gun. "Keep talking."

"They have your friend," Concho said, "but they killed my mustanging partner."

Ki closed the door. "Who are *they*?"

"Mind if I have a seat?" Concho asked, glancing toward a chair. "It's been a long, hard trail back here and I didn't think that I'd make it out with them two alive."

"What two?"

Concho took a seat. "I'm getting ahead of the story and need to back up a mite. Me and my friend Lance were mustanging up north of here when Jessie found us. She said she needed and was willing to pay for our help, so we took her to see some horse tracks she was interested in. By and by, the tracks eventually led us to a band of outlaws that were holding Amy Ross and another fella named Dan as their hostages."

Ki decided that the man was telling him the truth and put away his knife. "Why were they keeping Amy and this other man? For the Ross gold mine?"

"That's right," Concho said. "Anyway, Jessie insisted that we not only try to free the two, but also capture the entire outlaw band."

"How many?"

"There were six but now there can't be more than three or four. Trouble is, during the fight, my partner was shot to death and your lady friend was taken captive."

"Was she shot too?"

"I can't answer that one," Concho said. "All I know for sure is that they took her and when last I saw Jessie, she'd been knocked out cold."

Ki weighed this disturbing news for a moment and then he said, "I'm going to find them. Can you take me to the place where you had this fight?"

"Sure I could," Concho said, "but I ain't going to."

"Why not?"

"Because I'm out on my feet! My horse is shot and I need some rest."

"Very well, draw me a map."

"I guess I could do that," Concho said. "Mister, Jessie talked some about you and from what I heard, you're supposed to be one hell of a fighter. But you'll need a posse at your side, even though we whittled them sonsabitches down to just three or four. They're real mavericks and as cold-blooded as rattlesnakes. You can't take them alone."

"I'll be the judge of that," Ki said. "Just tell me where you attacked their camp."

Concho gave the samurai descriptions while Ki hurriedly packed his belongings. When the samurai was ready, Concho came to his own feet.

"You really going to go after them all by yourself?"

"I am," Ki said, moving toward the door.

Concho sighed. "I can't let you do that," he said.

"I don't need your help. I have your map."

"Jessie had it figured out where the Ross mine would be. My guess is that she'll lead the outlaws there, if she's still alive. It's the only card she has to play."

"Where did she think the mine was located?"

"I'll take you there if you'll pay me for fresh horse."

"I can't pay you, but Jessie will."

"When and if we can get her away from them alive. Those are long odds."

"Everything in the West is long odds," Ki said. "Help me and Jessie will generously repay you. Or stay and sleep. That's your decision, not mine."

"I'll help you but I need a fresh horse and an hour or two of sleep."

"No," Ki said. "Every hour is precious."

"I *have to have sleep,*" Concho said, "or I'll be no good to you. Two hours will be enough."

Ki weighted the proposition for several moments and then he nodded his head because he had a feeling that this young mustanger wanted revenge for the loss of his friend and, knowing the wild country of Central Nevada, would be very helpful in rescuing Jessie.

"All right," Ki said. "While you're sleeping, I'll interview Dan and Amy, then find and buy the best horse that I can on this short notice."

"You won't be sorry," Concho said. "I'll help you find Jessie and kill them murderin' sonsabitches."

"Good," Ki said as he went out the door to find and talk to Amy and the other man that had been rescued from the outlaws.

They were resting in the same hotel, but in a room on the first floor, and when Ki hurried inside to see Amy, he could scarcely believe how much suffering her face revealed. On the street, he doubted if he would even have recognized her.

"Ki!" she exclaimed. "Oh, Ki!"

The samurai did not like public displays of affection, but Amy seemed so overjoyed to see him that, in this case, he didn't really mind.

"I'm going to find Jessie," Ki said. "Anything that either one of you can tell me to help in the hunt would be appreciated."

"My name is Dan Smith," the other man said. "I never even had a chance to meet Miss Starbuck or the other mustanger, I believe his name was Lance, who lost so much while saving our lives."

Amy took Dan's arm. "He's a doctor, Ki. He saved me

162

after the stagecoach wreck. Then we had the bad luck to run into this terrible fellow named Modesto and his pack of wolves. The only reason we are still alive is that they believed I had to know the location of my father's gold mine."

"Do you?"

"No," Amy said. "But, of course, I couldn't tell them that."

"And even if she had," Dan interjected, "they wouldn't have believed her. They are convinced that there really is a fabulously rich gold mine out there waiting to be mined."

"They'll be brought to justice, one way or another," Ki said. "Concho is going to lead me to the place where you were freed from the outlaw camp."

"They won't be there any longer," Dan said. "They're hard, restless men. They'll be forcing Jessie to take them to the Ross mine."

"That's what Concho said," Ki told the pair. "And that's why we are leaving in a few hours."

"Be like finding a needle in a haystack, finding those men out in all that empty country," Dan said.

"We'll find them," Ki said with more confidence than he really felt. "We'll find them."

★

Chapter 21

Ki wasted no time in finding a top-grade horse for Concho. Then, he returned to his hotel room and prepared for the hunt that would take him to a showdown with the men who had killed George and Ken Ross as well as Concho's mustanging friend. When he was ready to leave, the samurai spent a few minutes in prayer and meditation. He reminded himself that he was a samurai and that he owed everything to Jessie and that it would be an honor to give his life in exchange for hers.

Exactly two hours after they had parted, Ki awoke the half-breed mustanger and said, "I have a good horse for you. You will be riding your own saddle."

"What about my horse?" Concho asked, looking groggy and haggard. "He's worth a lot of money."

"He is being well taken care of for however long we will be gone."

This explanation seemed to satisfy the mustanger. He rolled off the bed and pulled on his boots. "I might need to tie myself to the saddle in order not to fall asleep and pitch off to break my neck."

"If you wish," Ki said.

"I was only kidding," Concho said, dredging up a tired grin. "Don't worry, I can ride better in my sleep than most cowboys can fully awake. I can ride the wildest bronc and roll a cigarette at the same time. Don't worry about me holding you back. Did you get me a top horse?"

"As good as fifty dollars could buy," the samurai said.

"Well, that's a lot of money for a horse so I hope that you did not get completely skinned."

Ten minutes later, Concho was mounting a handsome palomino gelding. It was long and clean-limbed and deep in the chest. Despite his weariness, Concho was pleased. "You got me a good one and that pinto you're riding looks to be fast and sound. I think we ought to be overtaking those outlaws soon enough. Let's ride."

Ki was more than eager to leave Austin and head south. He and Concho left the livery and as soon as they were clear of the heavy foot and wagon traffic, they put their horses into an easy lope that would carry them far and fast.

Ki did not talk much under normal circumstances. A quiet, introspective man, he preferred to keep his thoughts to himself and to do whatever needed to be done. He knew that he was well prepared for a hard fight. He carried his bow and his quiver of arrows and they were unlike anything Concho had seen used by the native Paiute Indians.

Ki's bow was constructed of a light-colored layers of wood glued together and bound at several points with red silk thread. The bow's core was made of bamboo which had been strengthened by a special "fire treatment" that allowed the bow to become extremely light, flexible and strong. But perhaps most unusual, the bow was shaped in a way that almost defied logic until the bow was put to use and the observer noted with astonishment that it actually spun in a complete half circle the instant it was fired. When in the middle of a battle, Ki was capable of firing arrows even faster than the normal man could use a Winchester rifle.

"I sure wish we had rifles," Concho said more than once that first day out. "I never even thought to buy one and all I've got is my old Colt .44."

"That will be enough," Ki said.

"Maybe it would be if we both had shooters," Concho said, "but you brought that bow and arrows. They sure won't do is a lot of good if the lead starts flying."

Ki knew better. He had often proven that he was far more deadly with his bow, arrows, *shuriken* star blades and other Japanese weapons than a rifleman of the American West. But since this man would never have believed that, Ki said nothing. When the time came, he would let his actions speak instead of mere words.

They made camp that night and slept a solid seven hours, as much for Concho's sake as for that of their horses. They rode out at first light and were several miles closer to the outlaws by the time the sun struggled up in the eastern horizon.

"Are you a half-breed like me?" Concho asked later that morning.

When Ki chose not to answer, Concho said, "I'll bet you are. You're white and Oriental, aren't you?"

"Yes," Ki said. "My father was American, my mother was Japanese."

"Don't let that bother you," Concho said. "My mother

was Paiute and my father called himself a Spaniard. Maybe he was, but he'd been driven out of California when the Mexicans took over the Spanish ranchos. My father once had money, or so he used to tell me."

"What happened to him?"

"He was killed by a grizzly bear up in the Sierra Nevada Mountains when I was just ten years old. He roped the damn thing and was going to drag it down when his horse stepped in a badger hole and broke its leg. My father got pinned under the horse and couldn't get his rifle out. The bear killed both Father and his horse."

"I heard that the Spaniards used to rope grizzly bears and put them in with their Spanish bulls," Ki said. "I can't understand why."

"For the blood sport of it!" Concho explained. "They'd fight to the death. Most often the bear would kill three or four bulls before it would get gored and then weaken. My father said that one huge grizzly killed eight bulls before the last one got him down and put a horn through his heart."

"Are you a roper?" Ki asked.

Concho patted the sixty foot riata that was tied to his saddle. "I can play this thing like some men can play a banjo. I can make it dance on the air and land so softly over a mustang's neck that it doesn't even know that it's been caught."

"That's quite an art," Ki said. "I've tried to learn how to rope, but it isn't easy."

"Course it's not. And I'll bet that you can shoot that bow better'n an Indian. At least, I hope you can or we're going to be in big trouble."

"We will kill them all if they refuse to surrender," Ki vowed. "Too many men have died over the promise of

168

a gold mine that might not even exist."

They rode for another hour before Concho said, "I wish you'd have known my partner. Lance was a hell of a man. He didn't care about your pedigree. Didn't matter to him your color or nothing. The only thing that counted in Lance's opinion was how well you could ride, rope and catch wild horses. That's all he lived for."

"He sounds like a fine man. I'm sorry that he was killed."

"He was worth any twenty of the likes of that Modesto and his bunch," Concho said bitterly. "I'll never be able to find another partner like Lance."

"Maybe someone will show up."

"I don't suppose you'd like to learn how to catch mustangs, would you?"

Ki shook his head. "No," he said, appreciating what the younger man was offering. "But that's only because I've sworn to protect Miss Starbuck."

"You mean that's the only thing that you do? Like a body guard or something?"

"Or something," Ki said.

He pointed toward the distant hills that were corroding into a high plateau. "Have you any idea how much farther we might have to go before we overtake Jessie and her captors?"

"As a matter of fact," Concho said, "I think that I see a trace of something over on that hillside. Looks to me like the tracks of horses riding single file."

"Where?"

"Over there," Concho said, pointing.

When Ki followed the mustanger's finger, he saw the faint outline of tracks. "You have very keen eyes."

"It helps in my line of work," Concho said, wheeling his horse off to the right and setting spurs to its flanks.

They galloped for about three hundred yards cutting through the tall sage until they struck and climbed the side of the hill. Concho dismounted to study the tracks.

"Shod horses," he said.

"How many?"

"That's what I'm figuring out," Concho said. "The ground here is so rocky I can't really get a fix on it just yet."

The half-breed remounted his horse. "Let's ride along and follow these tracks for a couple of miles. Sooner or later, they'll come down on this hillside and cross softer ground. That's when I'll easily be able to tell how many horses there are."

Ki understood and, sure enough, in another half mile they hit a soft patch of ground and Concho didn't even have to dismount. "There are three horses and, from the depth of the imprints on a couple of them, I'd say they were being ridden double."

"It sounds like we've found the tracks of the men we're seeking," Ki said.

"I'm sure of it," Concho replied. "I've followed these same tracks before. It's Modesto and what is left of his gang, all right."

Ki felt an immense sense of relief, although it was not reflected on his face. All he needed was a chance to get into striking distance. Then, he would make saving Jessie's life his number one priority. That accomplished, he would deal with the outlaws and, if they chose not to surrender, he would show them no mercy.

★

Chapter 22

Jessie and Modesto stood at the crown of a tall, sage-covered mountain where they commanded a view of southern Nevada that stretched out for hundreds of miles. Just below them, the surviving outlaws squatted in the shade of their horses.

"Well," Modesto growled. "There's no gold mine and I'm going to have to kill you."

"Why"

"Because that's what I told my men I'd do. Now, if I were to go soft, I'd lose their respect."

Jessie could feel cold sweat trickling down her spine. She had run out of time and knew it.

"The Ross gold mine is down there someplace," Jessie said. "I told you it was about two days ride southeast of Austin, southwest of Eureka. It's got to be within ten miles of where we're standing."

"I don't see nothing but sage, sand, and rock," Modesto told her.

Jessie tried to keep the desperation out of her voice.

"But I see hills. And . . . and a faint track through the sage!"

"Where?"

"Look sharp," Jessie told the outlaw, "and you can just see it traced through that sage. In fact, there are a number of faint tracks, as if . . . as if someone were making a conscious effort to take a slightly different rail to their claim each time so as not to leave a clear marking. But they did, and we can see it from high up on this mountain."

Modesto squinted and leaned forward. "By Gawd," he said, unable to hide the mounting excitement in his voice, "I think I see what you mean!"

"Of course you do!" Jessie tried to slow her heartbeat. "And look at where those faint trails all converge. See that little hillock with the broken orange-colored rock?"

"Yeah."

"Do you notice something *different* about the rock surrounding that hill?"

Modesto's brow furrowed. "Can't say as I do."

"Well, I do," Jessie said. "The rock around that hill is also those same orange and red ferrous iron colors of the nearby hillock."

"Spell it out plain."

"What has happened," Jessie said, "is that someone has scattered their tailings over about an acre of land instead of dumping them in a pile that would attract attention from a wandering prospector."

"Gawdammit!" Modesto roared. "I think you're on to somethin', pretty lady!"

Jessie expelled a deep sigh of relief. She knew in her heart that she had actually found the Ross mine and that it would probably be rich with gold. And although it broke her heart to lead these murderers to a fortune,

Jessie also realized that she would have been shot—or worse—if she had not spotted the mine. In fact, she was quite sure that Modesto had intended to kill her within the next few minutes. She'd given them the mine, but in return she'd bought herself a little time. Time was life and there was always the possibility that, in the excitement of finding a fortune in gold, Jessie would realize an opportunity for escape.

"Let's go!" Modesto said, looking excited. "I think we've finally found the sonofabitch! George nor Ken would tell us, but we've found it anyway!"

The big man practically threw Jessie down the mountainside and it was all she could do to keep from tumbling headlong down to the horses and waiting men.

"We spotted it!" Modesto crowed to the others.

His excitement was like a current that passed instantly through the outlaws. They began to all shout questions at once until Modesto swung Jessie up into his saddle, then mounted behind, his left hand gathering the reins, his right encircling her small waist.

"The little lady here spotted the lost gold mine we've been tryin' to find. At least it had damn sure *better* be the Ross gold mine. Let's ride!"

Jessie had no choice but to hang on tight as the outlaws spurred their horses off the base of the mountain and began to gallop toward the distant point that she was certain marked the Ross gold mine.

The horses were blowing hard by the time they reached the site and, for a few awful minutes while the outlaws searched high and low for a tunnel or shaft, Jessie thought that she might actually have been wrong about the mine. But then one of the outlaws bellowed, "I found it! I found the sonofabitch!"

Everyone, including Jessie, followed to the place where he began to drag huge tumbleweeds away from a mine shaft. And even though the tumbleweeds were dead and sharp with stickers, the outlaws seemed to feel no pain as they tore them away.

"Gawdammit, he even stuffed the entrance of the tunnel with 'em," one of the men groused.

"Better these tumbleweeds than a damned dead and stinking burro!"

It seemed to take forever but probably took less than two minutes before all the tumbleweeds were pulled out of the mine's dark entrance.

"Me first!" Modesto called, lighting a match and crouching at the tunnel's entrance. "I want to be the first one to lay sight on a fortune in gold."

The outlaws were so crazed by gold fever that they all pushed in after Modesto and disappeared into the hillside. Jessie knew that their fever-pitch would never be greater than right now, at the moment of almost hysterical anticipation. Forgotten for only a few moments while the outlaws rushed inside the mine, she realized that this was her long-awaited chance.

Spinning on her heel, Jessie ran for the horses. There were only four and she meant to take every last one of them and leave these murderers stranded without rifles or water.

But the men's excitement had somehow affected the horses. Modesto's tall bay horse snorted and danced out of reach. Another of the animals trotted after it, also snorting and acting spooked.

"Dammit!" Jessie railed, more at herself than the horses. "Slow down!"

She managed to grab the reins of one horse, a runty

174

sorrel, the poorest and slowest animal of the lot. "Easy, easy," she crooned, smoothing her hand over the sorrel's muzzle as she led it toward the fourth horse, a buckskin.

The buckskin was an animal of quality and Jessie wanted that horse in the worst way. It wasn't quite as fast or strong as Modesto's horse, but then, even if he came after her, the outlaw leader carried a lot more weight and that might even out the slight difference between their horses.

"Easy now," Jessie crooned, leading the sorrel slowly forward, hand outstretched toward the buckskin. "I'm not going to hurt you. In fact, I'll even help you, if you help me."

The buckskin had a lot of pink and white ringing the black pupils of its eyes. It snorted and Jessie thought sure it was going to bolt and gallop off to join the other two horses. But it didn't.

"Easy," she crooned as she gathered the buckskin's reins up and then began to haul herself up into the saddle.

"Hey!" Modesto shouted as he suddenly emerged from the mine tunnel. "Gawddamn you!"

Jessie didn't even look back. The buckskin started to wheel and run, but Jessie had a firm grip on the saddlehorn and she was able to get a boot into the stirrup. A volley of gunfire erupted to shatter the still desert air and the buckskin faltered badly.

Jessie somehow managed to get her leg over the cantle, but she looked down and saw that the buckskin was mortally wounded. The poor animal had taken a bullet in the flanks and its stride was already beginning to deteriorate.

Jessie had no choice but to ride the dying buckskin into the ground in order to get out of pistol range. It broke her heart to hear the poor beast's grunts of agony as it ran until it collapsed. And when the buckskin fell, Jessie was ready. She yanked Modesto's Winchester out of its saddle scabbard and kicked out of her stirrups to hit the ground rolling. Coming to her feet, Jessie levered a shell into the rifle and knelt on one knee. She could see the outlaws trying to catch up their spooked horses. If they caught them, they would also have water and rifles. Then, Jessie knew that she would not be able to hold out against them for more than a few hours before they encircled and shot her to death.

"God forgive me," Jessie said as she began took aim on the runty little sorrel and pulled the trigger.

Her shot was not meant to kill the sorrel, but to spook it into a run. This Jessie accomplished. The little horse ran to join the other pair of horses that had bolted off and all three of them stopped and threw their heads to the wind.

"Go!" Jessie pleaded as she fired two more bullets that she hoped would kick up dirt right in front of the wary and confused saddle horses. "Run!"

Modesto and his men saw and understood Jessie's desperate game. They tried to reach the three horses before Jessie's rifle drove them off but failed. And when the three horses whirled and raced back in the direction of Austin, Jessie wanted to shout with joy because now her enemies were stranded on foot.

She went over to the dying buckskin and mercifully put the animal out of its misery. She removed a canteen and saddlebags with extra ammunition and then she began to walk after the fleeing horses.

Toward Austin and toward Ki.

★

Chapter 23

When Ki first saw Jessie, he could hardly believe his eyes. Jessie was riding a tall bay horse and leading two others. She was moving steadily along a ridge, and Ki could see that she kept looking back over her shoulder as if she were worried that she might be followed.

Ki and Concho sent their own horses into a gallop and when Jessie saw them, she waved and pushed her own horses into a shambling trot. Ki could see that she was dirty and looked thinner than usual, but the fact that Jessie could still smile after all that she had been through was remarkable.

"I wonder if Jessie killed them to the last man?" Concho shouted.

"We'll soon find out."

When they were reunited, Jessie said, "You are both a welcome sight, I'll tell you that for certain!"

"What happened to Modesto and his bunch?" Ki asked.

"We found Amy's gold mine. The one that her father

and brother were murdered for. That's where Modesto and his men are right now."

Jessie twisted around in her saddle and looked back south. "Unless they've already realized that they'll die without water and they had better not delay hiking out of that part of the country in order to find it."

"By damned, Jessie! You did it!" Concho exclaimed with unconcealed admiration. "You beat 'em!"

"It was as much gold fever as anything I did that proved their undoing. How far is it to Austin?" Jessie asked. "I'm been over so much country this past week that I'm not even sure where I am anymore."

"It's only a day's ride to the northwest," Ki said.

"And your wound?" Jessie asked, looking closely at the samurai.

"I'm fine." Ki rode over and placed his hand on Jessie's arm. "But you look like you've been marching through hell."

"I think I have."

Concho chuckled. "They'll never make it out of there without horses or water. All we have to do is to wait a couple days and the desert will pay 'em back for killing George, Ken and my partner, Lance."

"Uh-uh," Jessie said. "As much as they deserve to die, we can't let them. We'll go back and . . ."

"No," Ki said. "*You'll* go back. I'll round them up and do what I can for them."

"Why!" Concho shouted. "They're the worst bunch of murderers in . . ."

"They'll be tried for murder and they'll hang," Jessie said, cutting off Concho's strong protest.

The mustanger shook his head. "I refuse to even lift a finger to help them."

"I'll go alone," Ki said. "Jessie, can you spare a couple

178

of those canteens full of water that I see tied to the extra horses?"

"Sure. In fact, take the extra horses. But I'm warning you, Ki, those men are treacherous and just because they might be afoot and half dead of thirst doesn't mean that they'll meekly surrender or thank you for coming back to save them from a slow and horrible death."

"I know that."

Concho's jaw dropped. "But they have pistols, don't they!"

"They do," Jessie said. "Ki, maybe . . ."

But the samurai wasn't listening. "Concho, take Jessie to see Dr. Alton. I'll be along in a few days."

"You're crazy!" Concho swore. "You're just going to get yourself killed for no damn good reason. That bunch murdered a lot of good men just to steal themselves a gold mine. Let it become their grave!"

Ki wasn't the kind of man to argue. He knew that Jessie could not, in good conscience, allow the four outlaws to die of thirst. Therefore, he would at least attempt to save them.

So he rode away following Jessie's path and determined to give Modesto and the outlaws a chance they really didn't deserve.

The outlaws must have found a spring someplace nearby or even a water well that the Ross men had dug because they were in good health and working the mine when Ki came in sight of them late the following afternoon. Ki dismounted and hid his horse. Taking his bow and arrows, he crept up closer and discovered that Modesto and his men were preparing to leave in order to get badly needed horses and supplies.

Modesto was giving orders. "We'll cover the damned

179

thing up with tumbleweeds just like we found it and then we'll pack out what gold we can carry."

"That Starbuck woman will bring half of Austin back here with her for protection and we'll never have another chance at this gold mine."

"I know that," Modesto growled. "But I'm toting about seventy pounds of pure gold and high grade ore that I figure ought to bring me about three thousand dollars. Each of you boys has packed nearly the same. So I say we take what we can carry and get out of here before trouble arrives. Even with what we can carry we'll still be wealthy men and we can always come back and try to get some more."

"There's no other choice," Rafe Cowley said bitterly. "Once that Starbuck woman escaped, the game was up. We should have killed her when we had the chance."

"No sense cryin' over it now," Modesto said as the last tumbleweed was pulled into place and all sign of their presence was brushed away. "We're just damn lucky we found not only gold, but a spring with good water. Let's go. We need to travel as many miles as we can before tomorrow morning's heat."

Ki let them go. The sun was dying in the west and the fierce heat of the desert was finally beginning to subside. He waited until they were well out of sight and then he returned to his pinto. He would follow the outlaws until sometime in the predawn hours when they would be drugged by lack of sleep, exhausted and their guard was down. Then, he would confront them and either bring them to trial, or do his best to kill every last one.

★

Chapter 24

Ki looked up at the stars and judged it to be about three o'clock in the morning. The outlaws were still walking north, but under their heavy loads of ore and the still oppressive heat, they were moving very slowly and were probably suffering from thirst. Earlier on, they had been in good spirits, talking and bragging about how they would spend their money. But the last few hours, they'd become very quiet and twice, someone had suggested that they stop and rest during what remained of the hot night.

"There'll be no stopping until the blast of the morning sun gets to us," Modesto had ordered. "We're almost out of water and we can't afford to lose a minute or we'll wind up as rich corpses."

Since that declaration, the outlaws had suffered in grim silence. Now, Ki decided it was time to act. He dismounted and tied his horse, then took his black and loose-fitting ninja outfit from his saddlebags. He dressed quickly, checked his bow and weapons, then melted into the semi-darkness.

Ten minutes later, he had circled around in front of the outlaws and when they came shuffling up through the sage, Ki appeared in their path and said, "You are all under arrest for murder."

Modesto's jaw dropped. He stared at the black apparition which held a bow and an arrow and blocked his path. Modesto blinked as if he were sure that his eyes had betrayed him.

"Drop your weapons and you will not die," the samurai felt compelled to order.

Modesto leaned forward, eyes straining in the darkness. "By Gawd," he whispered, "you're the same one that we shot down in Austin!"

"And you're the one that lured me out into the street so that your man could get a clean shot," Ki said.

Modesto dropped his pack and it fell heavily to the dirt. "Well," he said with a quick shrug of his shoulders, "I guess I might as well finish up the job."

Modesto's hand dug for the handle of his six-gun but Ki was already plucking a *shuriken* star blade from his tunic. Ki's arm shot forward and the star blade spun like polished silver across the distance that separated the enemies. It made a dull sound like a meat cleaver when it hacks a side of beef only it struck the flesh and bone of Modesto's forehead. Two razor-sharp points of the *shuriken* pierced Modesto's thick skull and penetrated his brain.

Modesto grunted, hand twitching on his gunbutt. He staggered backward into his men and collapsed. The three remaining outlaws, not having heard a gunshot, did not know what had happened. They went for their guns and Ki knew that he did not have enough time to put an arrow in them all. So he shot the nearest one through the heart and then he attacked and gutted the next man with the sharp tip of his bow.

The last outlaw did manage to get off a shot but it was wild and by that time, Ki had retrieved his *nunchaku*, the two seven-inch sticks which were attached by a strip of braided horsehair. The *nunchaku* he preferred were the *han-kei* or "half-sized" version and now they whirled more deadly than spinning razors as they struck the remaining outlaw with crushing force in the throat. The man's gun bucked twice spilling harmless bullets into the earth and then he grabbed his crushed windpipe and collapsed.

Ki stepped over the man who could not breathe and whose heels began to drum the earth faster and faster. He was choking to death and there was nothing the samurai could do to save his worthless life now.

The samurai turned his back on the dead outlaws and returned to his horse. He would load the heavy packs of gold and lead the animal back to Austin.

At least, Ki thought, Amy Ross would finally have her father and brother's accursed Nevada gold.

Watch for

LONE STAR AND THE TEXAS TORNADO

148th novel in the exciting LONE STAR series
from Jove

Coming in December!

From the Creators of Longarm!

Featuring the beautiful Jessica Starbuck
and her loyal half-American half-
Japanese martial arts sidekick Ki.